P9-CRD-853

For the Record

by MONIQUE POLAK

Owlkids Books

Owlkids Books acknowledges the financial support of the Canada Council for the Arts, the Ontario Arts Council, the Government of Canada through the Canada Book Fund (CBF) and the Government of Ontario through the Ontario Creates Book Initiative for our publishing activities.

Published in Canada by
Owlkids Books Inc.,
1 Eglinton Avenue East,
Toronto, ON M4P 3A1

Published in the US by
Owlkids Books Inc.,
1700 Fourth Street,
Berkeley, CA 94710

Library of Congress Control Number: 2021942148

Library and Archives Canada Cataloguing in Publication
Title: For the record / by Monique Polak.
Names: Polak, Monique, author.
Identifiers: Canadiana (print) 20210255919 | Canadiana (ebook) 20210255927 | ISBN 9781771474375 (hardcover) | ISBN 9781771475518 (EPUB) | ISBN 9781771475525 (PDF)
Classification: LCC PS8631.O43 F665 2022 | DDC jC813/.6—dc23

Edited by Sarah Harvey
Designed by Alisa Baldwin

Manufactured in Altona, MB, Canada, in January 2022, by Friesens
Job #278699

A B C D E F

For Lesley Lacate, whose
oh-so-wise and ever-so-kind voice
I hope to hear forever in my head.

CHAPTER ONE

Saturday, Sept. 15

1. He let B have WHITE bread with jam for breakfast. (I refused to eat it.)

2. He didn't remind us to put on sunscreen before we went to play in the backyard.

3. He yelled. His exact words were: "Could you two keep it down? I'm trying to get some work done!" His voice was so loud B started to cry.

4. He ignored the rule about B's 7 p.m. bedtime. Also, he didn't make us floss. (Not flossing is bad for your teeth and can lead to heart disease. Okay, for heart disease, you probably have to forget to

floss every night for fifty years ... but good habits matter.)

5. I just checked and it's now one hour and four minutes past B's bedtime. He's letting her stay up to watch a movie. When I warned him that B will be cranky tomorrow, he tweaked my ear and said, "Can I ask you something, Justine? Who's in charge here? You or me?"

I hate living in two places.

Let me try that again.

I despise it.

Despise is a way better word to describe my feelings. I also like how *despise* sounds. It's got way more hate in it than the word *hate*.

Most mornings, when I first wake up, I'm not even sure where I am.

So I came up with a system. If I hear birds, like I do now, I know I'm at Dad's house in Montreal West. There's also the peeling wallpaper with pink flowers, which Dad says he's going to tear off. Then he'll paint the room whatever color I want. Only something tells me I'm going to be looking at peeling wallpaper for the rest of my life. The to-do list on

Dad's fridge keeps getting longer, and hardly anything ever gets crossed off.

I can't hear birds at Mom's condo in Saint-Lambert because her windows are soundproof. And the walls are off-white. Mom read somewhere that off-white walls have a calming effect. (Peeling wallpaper definitely doesn't.)

Dad's floors creak, so I tiptoe to the bathroom. I want Bea to sleep in. Otherwise she turns into Crab-Bea.

Dad's in the bathroom, shaving. "Morning, sweetheart," he says, as he drags the razor in a smooth line across his chin.

"Not so loud, Dad," I whisper. "Bea's asleep. And I need to pee . . . if you don't mind."

Dad keeps shaving. "Nearly done," he says in a voice that's only a touch lower.

"Nearly going to pee on your floor."

"Ew." Dad steps away from the sink and out to the hallway. Of course he forgets to close the bathroom door, so I do it for him.

Dad's house has only one bathroom. It's one of the reasons Mom and Maître Pépin, her lawyer, are trying to reduce the amount of time Bea and I spend here. Twelve-year-olds like me shouldn't have to share a bathroom with a grown man. When Mom bought the condo, she made sure it had two bathrooms.

"Bea!" I hear Dad calling. "Time to wake up!"

So much for letting her sleep in.

"I've got a surprise for you girls today!" Dad adds.

I hear Bea yawn, then ask Dad about the surprise.

I want to know about the surprise too. So after I brush my teeth, I go to Bea's room. Dad is sitting at the end of her bed. There's shaving cream on his lip.

Bea rubs her eyes. "Tell me!" she says. "Tell me the surprise."

"Then it wouldn't be a surprise. I thought you loved surprises."

"I do! I do! Does Marry know?" Bea asks.

Mariella (Bea calls her Marry) is the one really good thing about having to spend every second weekend and each Wednesday night at Dad's. She's our big sister. Half sister to be exact, though she feels whole to me.

Mariella's out for a run. I know because if she was here, I'd hear her laughing or chatting on the phone with one of her hundreds of friends. Mariella is an expert at making friends and having fun. She runs every morning, even in February when it's so cold her eyelashes stick together. When we're apart and I picture Mariella, that's how I see her: eyelashes covered in snowflakes, laughing.

"Nope," Dad says. "I haven't told Mariella. You might not know this, but even fifteen-year-olds like surprises."

I tap Dad's shoulder. "There's shaving cream on your lip."

He licks the shaving cream off—and eats it. Which can't be healthy.

"Dad!" I say.

"Justine!" he says with a grin.

"Is the surprise candy?" Bea asks.

"Nope," Dad says.

"Candy's bad for your teeth," I say. Bea isn't listening.

"Please, Daddy," Bea says. "Tell us the surprise."

"How about I give you a clue? We're going someplace special. To get something special. Something my three girls are gonna love."

"Going to," I say, even though my friend Solange says I need to stop correcting people's grammar.

I help Bea into her purple overalls. She loves everything purple. Purple grapes (she won't eat the green ones), purple crayons, purple pajamas, purple ponytail holders.

When we come downstairs, Dad's in the kitchen. Mariella's back. Her T-shirt is soaked and her face is shiny with sweat. Even without makeup and her usual gold hoop earrings, Mariella is beautiful. She has silky black hair and long, slim legs.

My hair's boring-brown and frizzy as a dandelion. It's just my luck that of Dad's three daughters, I'm the one who inherited his frizz and also his chunky build, which is even worse than the frizz.

When I was little, I used to hope that one day I'd wake up looking like Mariella, but now I've accepted that's never going to happen. The only physical trait the two of us share is a small brown beauty mark in the exact same spot—just above our lips on the right side. The dermatologist offered to remove Mariella's, but she told him no way, that it's part of who she is—and that it connects her to me.

"I could've sworn we still had bread," Dad mumbles to himself. He hasn't figured out that I hid the white bread in one of the bottom drawers.

"I think there's shredded wheat in the pantry." I say this like it's no big deal.

"Shredded wheat?" Dad's Adam's apple jiggles. Shredded wheat is my mom's favorite.

"No added sugar or salt," Dad and I say at the exact same time. We say it the way Mom used to. Mom's great at imitations, and she's especially good at old commercials, which is where the shredded wheat voice comes from. Dad and I both start to laugh. Only I swallow mine before it's completely out, and cross my arms over my chest. I can't explain why I don't want to laugh with my dad. I just don't.

Half an hour later, we pile into his SUV. Mariella sits up

front because she's the eldest. She pulls down the visor so she can look in the mirror while she dabs on silver-pink lip gloss. Mariella says you can be sporty and smart, but also into makeup. She says basically a person can be whatever they want to be—that that's the secret to happiness. It's cool having a big sister who thinks about that kind of stuff.

Dad hums as he reverses out of the driveway. I'm waiting for him to remind me and Mariella to put on our seat belts. Except he doesn't.

"Dad," I say. "You forgot something. How about I give you a clue? It's something important."

Dad stops humming. "Seat belts!" he calls out like he's a participant on *Jeopardy*. "What would I do without you, Justine? You're better than the police. Because you don't give tickets." Dad cracks up at his own joke.

Dad and Mariella pull their seat belts across their chests. Then once I've checked that Dad buckled Bea into her car seat properly, I put on my seat belt too.

When we get onto the Décarie Expressway, the sunken highway that leads in and out of Montreal, Mariella says she thinks she knows where we're going.

Bea bops up and down in her seat. "Where? Where are we going, Marry?"

Dad turns his head and shoots Mariella a look. I have

to remember to add that to my notes: *While driving on the expressway, D took his eyes off the road.*

Even I get excited when Dad exits at Rue Jean-Talon, turns a corner and pulls up in front of a redbrick building.

"I knew it!" Mariella fist pumps the air. "The SPCA!"

Bea is bopping double-time as she tries to read the red-and-black sign outside. "*S* . . ." she says. "*P* . . ." For a four-year-old, Bea's a really good reader. We read to her a lot. Mom says we're helping Bea's brain develop something called *neural pathways*.

"Are we getting a dog?" Mariella asks Dad as we climb out of the SUV.

"I was thinking more along the lines of a cat," Dad says. "Cats are lower maintenance. You don't need to walk them or bag their poop during a blizzard."

"Yay!" Bea says. "I love cats. I love how they purr." She makes a purring sound as she tugs on my sleeve. "Daddy says we're getting a cat!"

The inside of the SPCA smells like a mix of pee and cleaning fluid—and something else. If sadness had a smell, this is what it would smell like.

The others don't seem to notice the odor. Bea is running down the corridor where the cats are, peering into the metal cages and calling out her opinion of every one. "This one has patches!" "This one's so fat!" "This one's the color of caramel." "There are three kitties in here!"

Mariella is taking her time, stopping in front of each cage to read the index card with information about the cat. She sneezes twice. I hope she isn't catching an end-of-summer cold. Those last forever—probably because of the weather. September in Montreal can mean a heat wave Monday, sweaters and wool socks by Tuesday.

Dad is talking to a technician. "These cats have all been vaccinated," I hear her tell him. "The females have been spayed and the males neutered."

"Justine," Bea calls. "Come see this one!"

I expect to see a fluffy kitten. So I take a sharp breath when my eyes land on the animal Bea wants me to see. It's a full-grown gray cat with only one eye. Where the other eye should be is a patch of wrinkled pinkish-gray skin.

"What do you think happened to him?" Bea whispers. She's usually a loud talker. She probably doesn't want to remind the cat of whatever injured its eye.

Mariella, Dad and the technician come to see the one-eyed cat. Mariella finds the answer to Bea's question on the index card outside the cage and reads the information out loud: "Male cat, approximately three years old. Found abandoned in downtown Montreal. Right eye missing, probably lost during a fight. Otherwise, in excellent health. Friendly."

I try to imagine this one-eyed cat wandering downtown, slinking between the office workers, shoppers and tourists who crowd the sidewalks. Did he ever follow the steps down to one of the metro stations and hear the buskers play music? Did he find mice to eat or did people give him scraps?

"There aren't a lot of people willing to adopt a one-eyed cat," the technician tells us.

"What happens if no one adopts him?" Mariella asks her.

The technician doesn't answer. Instead, she shrugs. I'm pretty sure that means the cat will get put down.

"Can we get him?" Bea asks. "Please, Daddy!"

The four of us don't usually agree on stuff: I like it when Dad's AC is on high; Mariella likes the windows open. Dad and Bea love watching comedies; Mariella and I are into teen dramas.

But this time, we all agree.

That's how we end up adopting Sheldon.

Dad thinks we should call him Cyclops—after a one-eyed giant from Greek mythology. But Bea is the one who comes up with his name. It's short for Sheldon J. Plankton from *SpongeBob SquarePants*.

Like our new cat and Cyclops, Sheldon Plankton only has one eye.

CHAPTER TWO

Sunday, Sept. 16

1. He let B sprinkle sugar on her strawberries. When I told him sugar is poison, he laughed and said, "Hemlock and arsenic are poison. Last time I checked, sugar wasn't on the poison list."

2. M is catching a cold. He didn't say ANYTHING when we were all sitting in the kitchen and M coughed WITHOUT COVERING HER MOUTH. (He should have at least made her use the inside of her elbow like they make us do at school.)

3. He didn't do any reading with B all weekend. Instead, they watched TWO movies together. Doesn't he care about B's neural pathways?

Something about the semicircular driveway in front of Mom's condo makes me happy. It could be the shape, which reminds me of a rainbow, or that it's bordered by bright-red flowers called impatiens. And of course when I see it, I know Mom's nearby. The two of us have always been super close. It's like I feel her feelings. Which doesn't happen to me with most people.

When we get to the driveway, Dad turns off the engine and steps out of the SUV.

"Uh, we can go in by ourselves," I try telling him. Mom gets upset when she lays eyes on him. *Lays eyes*. Those are her words. Whenever she says that, I think of a chicken laying eggs. Like it's something Mom sometimes has to do, even if it's hard for her.

Dad leans down and hugs us both at the same time. It's a good thing he has long arms. He adds an extra squeeze before letting go. "I'll see you Wednesday after school. Right, Officer?" he says to me.

I can't help laughing when he calls me that. "Right."

Bea grabs Dad's knee. "Bye, Daddy. I miss you already. And Mariella. And Sheldon. Sheldon the most."

Dad and I chuckle when she says that. Bea is always cracking us up. She's one of those people who are the funniest when they're not trying to be funny. "Maybe we can Skype before Wednesday," he tells her. "That way you and Sheldon can purr at each other—and talk tuna."

"I don't think that'll work," I say. "We get limited screen time on school nights."

"Lemme talk to your mom," Dad says. "Maybe we can come to some sort of agreement."

I don't say what I'm thinking: First of all, it's *let me*, not *lemme* (I'm trying to take Solange's advice about correcting people); and secondly, I don't think my parents will ever agree about anything. I'm pretty sure that's why they got divorced in the first place. Because somewhere along the way, they stopped agreeing.

Dad loved the house in the Eastern Townships; Mom missed the city. Dad wanted to speak to us in French; Mom thought our being really good at English mattered more—and that Bea and I could learn French at school. That was another thing they didn't agree about: schools. Dad believed in public; Mom said private schools gave kids advantages—smaller classes, and the opportunity to mix with kids from *good* families. By *good*, I'm pretty sure she meant *rich*. Which we aren't. At least not anymore.

There must've been a time when Mom and Dad got along—or they wouldn't have gotten married in the first place—but I can't remember it. All I remember are the fights, and how I wished I could run away, only there was nowhere to go except for Darlene and Will's house down the road, and I couldn't stay there forever.

Mariella says the arguments got worse after Dad's company tanked and money became a problem. When Dad started out in e-commerce, he was one of the only software engineers helping companies sell their products online. He was even named Montreal's Entrepreneur of the Year! Mom met him at the banquet supper. Nana (Mom's mom) told me the story. It was love at first sight. Nana says Mom fell for Dad's sense of humor, and his European charm. And that he fell for her beauty and how organized she is.

Lots of engineers ended up working in e-commerce, and eventually that edged Dad out of his job. But now he's looking into starting a new kind of online business. Only he hasn't figured out that part yet.

I'd never tell Mariella that Mom says she feels sorry for Dad because he'll probably never figure it out—that he rode the wave while it lasted, that all he'll ever be able to get is contract work and that he'll never make a good living again.

Mom is waiting in the lobby. "Hello, my two sweethearts," she says, looking up at us from her phone. "Now why am I not surprised that you two are ten minutes late? For as long as I've known him, that man has always been ten minutes late." She sighs. I'm about to say she could try coming ten minutes late too, and then she wouldn't have to get annoyed, but Bea interrupts my thought.

"We got a cat. His name is Sheldon. I named him for Sheldon Plankton. Our Sheldon only has one eye, like Sheldon Plankton." Once Bea starts talking, it's hard for her to stop. "He's three years old. A little younger than me. I'm four," Bea says, lifting four fingers in the air.

Mom puts her hand over her mouth and shakes her head. "A cat with one eye? The poor thing! Where in the world did you find a cat with only one eye?"

"At the SPCA," I tell her. "He's super cute. He even purrs in his sleep. After a while, you stop noticing his eye."

"Thank goodness for that. But I know what you mean. When I was a girl, there was a cat named Trixie on our street, and she only had three—" Mom looks at Bea and stops herself. "She was the sweetest thing. Are you sure this new cat of yours doesn't have fleas?" Mom inspects the back of Bea's neck, checking for bites. "I'm always so glad to have you two back," she continues, not waiting for an answer. As we climb onto the elevator, she gathers the two of us close.

It's normal for parents to worry about their kids. But Mom worries more than the average mother. Things were really bad two years ago when she and Dad first split up. She couldn't sleep and she hardly ate. It was Darlene, Mom's best friend, who dragged Mom to the doctor. When she got back, Mom sat me down and explained that she had something called anxiety. She said the doctor recommended yoga and breathing exercises, and gave her special pills to make sleeping easier.

When I told Darlene how worried I was about Mom, Darlene said she thought Mom probably shouldn't have told me about her anxiety in the first place. That it was "TMI." But I'd have figured it out, even if I didn't know the word for it.

I know for a fact Mom's been having trouble sleeping again. Because if I get up to pee in the middle of the night, her light is often on. And sometimes I hear her making tea at like three in the morning. When I asked her if the sleeping pills weren't working, she told me she'd stopped taking them. She said they made her feel groggy during the day.

Now any time she has circles under her eyes or leaves food on her plate, I'm the one who worries.

Bea and I love the elevators at the condo. The walls and ceilings are made of mirrors, so we see our reflections everywhere. When it's just us, we do crazy dance moves and make weird faces.

"Bea," Mom asks, "did he work on your English reading with you?"

Though I'm sure Bea knows who *he* is, I answer for her. "He didn't do any reading with Bea. None at all." As soon as I say it, I feel this stab of guilt for turning Dad in, but then my eyes meet Mom's. When she nods at me, the guilty feeling starts to go away. Something about Mom's nod makes me feel very grown-up and responsible.

"We were too busy taking care of Sheldon," Bea says. "Besides, I'm a very good English reader."

"That's because you practice your English reading," Mom tells her. "People only get good at things if they practice."

Bea doesn't want to talk about reading. She tugs on the sleeve of Mom's shirt. "Can I FaceTime Sheldon later? Please?"

Mom sighs. "Tomorrow's a school day, Beatrice. So I'm afraid there won't be any FaceTiming tonight."

The elevator makes a soft ping when it stops, and the mirrored doors open on the eighth floor. A tall woman in a velour housecoat, carrying a striped beach towel, gets on.

I'm standing by the floor selection buttons, so I tap PH. The pool is on the penthouse level.

"Thanks, dear," the woman says. "What lovely girls," she says to Mom.

"Why, thank you." The way Mom says it makes me happy. As if nothing in the world matters to her more than being our mom.

Mom is the hardest-working, smartest and most devoted person I know.

The elevator stops on the eleventh floor. Mom scoops Bea up in her arms. "Enjoy your swim," she tells the woman as the elevator doors open. "You're an inspiration. I should get back to swimming too. I used to swim a lot when—"

The woman waits for Mom to finish her sentence, but Mom doesn't. "In that case," the woman says, "maybe I'll see you in the pool."

"Say goodbye, girls."

"Goodbye," Bea and I say together.

CHAPTER THREE

I really want a cellphone.

If I had one I could text my friends and Mariella whenever I felt like it, and I could look stuff up online. But Mom's against kids my age having their own phones. She says kids with cellphones are more likely to turn into couch potatoes. I tried telling her Mariella got one when she was twelve, and she's no couch potato, but that didn't help my case.

"You are not Mariella," Mom pointed out (as if I hadn't figured that out). "Besides, if you ask me, Mariella is spoiled rotten."

I nearly said I hadn't asked her, and that there's nothing rotten about Mariella, but I didn't want to cause trouble.

Mom and Leonor, Mariella's mom, aren't friends. Even though, when you think about it, they have something in common since they both got divorced from Dad.

Leonor was Dad's first wife. He and Leonor met when he was on vacation in Portugal. "He brought her home like a souvenir," I once heard Mom tell Darlene. "And even after all these years, the woman still sounds like she never left Lisbon."

Personally, I like Leonor's accent—sometimes it sounds like she's singing, not talking—and she's always been nice to me. Once, before Bea was born, when Mom and Dad were going to a wedding and couldn't find a babysitter for me, Leonor let me spend the night at her place with her and Mariella. I still remember being excited and nervous at the same time about sleeping over at their apartment. I remember how, when we were in the car, Mom and Dad sang "Here Comes the Bride" to make me laugh. That night, Leonor let Mariella and me make a fort from cardboard boxes, and we ate *natas*, little Portuguese custard tarts, for supper. *Natas* are a dessert, but Leonor said they're full of egg yolks and that on special occasions (like my being there), it's okay to skip the main course and have dessert instead.

If I had a phone, I could text Mariella anytime I wanted to. Instead, I have to text her on our home computer, which I'm only permitted to use twice a day: once for ten minutes in the morning, and then for fifteen minutes an hour before bedtime. Mom read this study that said screen time in the forty minutes before bed makes it harder to fall asleep.

This morning, I get on the computer to text Mariella.

How's your cold?

I can see from the gray dots on the screen that Mariella is writing back. Even those gray dots make me happy. I love having a big sister.

All gone.

Yay, I write back. *Did you run?*

Leaving now. Can't wait to see you Wednesday, sis.

Mom comes into the den, where the computer is, with her watering can. "What's making you smile like the Cheshire Cat?" she asks as she pours a little water into the saucers underneath her African violets.

I don't tell her that I love when Mariella calls me *sis*. She would probably remind me that Mariella is not my *real* sister. That I only have one *real* sister. "Nothing much," I answer.

"Hmm," Mom says.

Mom could be one of those people who get paid to organize other people's stuff. She hates clutter, so every single thing in the condo has its spot. Keys go on the key rack, and the spices in the spice drawer are arranged alphabetically. There's a slot on her desk for unread mail and another slot for mail she's opened but still needs to deal with.

Mom's an executive assistant at one of Montreal's biggest advertising agencies. At last year's family Christmas party, her boss, Monsieur Loisel, told me *he* works for Mom. "Most people don't know it, but your mother runs New and Improved Ads. I just do what she tells me." The way he said it made me think he wasn't really joking.

I nearly told Monsieur Loisel that's how it works at the condo too. He'd have laughed, but then I realized Mom was standing nearby and she might not have appreciated the joke.

When I walk into the kitchen, there are two bowls of steel-cut oats and almond milk waiting on the counter for Bea and me. Also two spoons, and two half oranges, cut into sections. Our lunches are ready too, lined up as neatly as the magnets on Mom's fridge. There's a rainbow and a *J* on my brown bag; Bea's has a drawing of a smiling bumblebee. (Mom could've been an artist.) She's made herself lunch too. Sometimes she goes out with people from work, but she says she prefers quiet time at her desk, and besides, most restaurant food has too much salt and fat.

Mom and Darlene talk every morning. Mom says they're soul sisters. Bea and I are eating oats when Mom's soul sister phones. Mom goes into her bedroom to take the call. But I can still hear her end of the conversation.

"Text me as soon you get home," I hear Mom say. Darlene must be going on some secret mission. I'm glad Mom's there for her.

There's a pause, then Mom says, "They're fine. They're always a handful when they get back after a weekend with him. What I haven't told you yet is that he took them to the SPCA and adopted a one-eyed cat. Yes, you heard me right. The poor thing has only one eye. Frankly, I'm concerned that being exposed to an animal like that could be traumatic, especially for the little one—" Mom drops her voice, and then she stops speaking altogether. Darlene is giving her opinion, which can take a while.

I don't know why Mom said we're a *handful* after we've been with Dad. It's true that last night, Bea started kicking when Mom lay down to read with her. And maybe Mom minded when I wouldn't say why I was smiling before. But that isn't exactly being a handful.

After breakfast, she drops us off. This year, Bea goes to the pre-K in the building next to my school, which makes things pretty simple. Then Mom heads to her office in Place Ville Marie, the city's most famous skyscraper. At night, the rotating beacon on its roof lights up the sky over all of Montreal.

"I've been thinking ahead to Christmas presents," Mom says. Leave it to her to plan for Christmas in September!

Bea bops up and down in her seat. "I love Christmas. What are you getting me?"

When Mom laughs, something lightens in my chest. She's been so serious lately. Especially when we get back from Dad's.

"Actually, Beatrice, I was thinking about a present for Nana and Gramps."

"Oh." Bea sounds disappointed.

"I want to give them a family portrait—of the three of us. Of course, we'd have to get our hair styled." Mom winks at me in the rearview mirror. "I might even let you wear a little makeup, Justine."

"You're kidding."

"Would I kid about something like that?" Mom asks.

I shake my head. Come to think of it, there aren't too many things Mom would kid about these days.

She thinks it's inappropriate for girls under the age of sixteen to wear makeup. She also says girls focus too much on their looks—that there's plenty of time for that later in life.

Mom never says anything about Mariella's makeup when she runs into her, but she doesn't have to. I always know when Mom disapproves of something.

"Just for once," Mom says.

"Can I wear makeup too? Like Justine and Marry?" Bea asks.

"Maybe a smidge of lip gloss," Mom tells her.

"Wow," Bea says to herself. "I'm allowed a smidge of lip

gloss. And I have a cat named Sheldon. I'm a very lucky little girl."

ooo

Later that morning, Mr. Farber tells us his job isn't just to teach grade six English, math and science. He says this year, he's also going to teach us how to learn, which is more important than any one subject.

Solange, who sits in front of me, is doodling on the cover of her textbook. Solange is obsessed with inventing girl superheroes. Her latest has ski goggles, fairy wings and a dragon's tail. Our friend Jeannine, who sits next to her, is checking out Solange's drawing.

Mr. Farber is always saying how kids learn in different ways. Solange is definitely what's called a visual learner. That's why he lets her doodle in class. But no matter which kind of learner you are, Mr. Farber says you need to know how to take good notes.

I put down my eraser I'd been fiddling with.

"One of the things students do wrong is write down every single word a teacher says. For instance, if I told you my wife's name is Fanny and we've been married for seventeen years, do you think you should include that in your notes?"

Jeannine raises her hand. "Only if you're going to ask us your wife's name on the pop quiz."

Everyone laughs, and one boy gives Jeannine a thumbs-up.

"Do you think that's likely, Jeannine?" Mr. Farber asks.

Jeannine gives her ponytail a shake. "Uh, no, I guess not. Sir."

"Exactly. The secret to successful note-taking is being selective. Good note-takers listen for what's most important."

I nod. Not just because I think Mr. Farber's right, but also because it means I take good notes.

Mr. Farber notices. "Justine, I see you agree with me."

"Yes," I say. Now I think of something else. "Don't good note-takers also need to *observe* stuff?" Like how I observed my dad letting Bea have white bread and letting her stay up past her bedtime.

"The way I observed you nodding just now?" Mr. Farber asks.

"Exactly."

When Mr. Farber laughs, I can see the silver fillings at the back of his mouth. "That's a useful point. Thank you, Justine, for adding to our discussion. I'd say you have the makings of an excellent note-taker."

Even if he is observant, Mr. Farber doesn't notice when

Solange tilts her head and mouths the word *suck-up* at me.

"FYI," I tell Solange at recess, "I'm not a suck-up."

"You sure had a lot to say about taking notes," Jeannine chimes in. "I was worried we'd miss recess."

"I'm into taking notes," I tell my friends. "But for the record, I'm also into recess."

CHAPTER FOUR

"Why can't Marry be in the photo too?" Bea asks Mom.

We're at the photo studio. It's on Westminster Avenue in Montreal West, not far from Dad's place. Like Bea, I wish Mariella was with us.

Mom is wearing her black-and-white checked shirt with a black skirt. Bea and I are in matching white shirts with gold buttons, and black pants. I could've argued when Mom said she wanted Bea and me to match. What twelve-year-old wants to dress the same as her four-year-old sister? But I could tell from the way Mom's breathing was speeding up that she was getting anxious.

Plus she did take us to get our hair done at the salon she goes to, and she let me break the no-makeup rule.

The walls in the waiting area are decorated with giant blow-ups of the photographer's work. A bride and groom gaze into each other's eyes, laughing as they stand under an umbrella, heavy rain pelting down around them. A family of four, all wearing denim shirts and white jeans, are lined up in a row like Russian nesting dolls. An old woman sits in a pine rocking chair, holding a toothless baby on her lap.

The photos are under glass and for a second I catch my reflection next to the rocking chair. My white shirt looks dorky, but my hair is perfect—totally frizz-free. And I can see a little of the makeup Mom put on for me—a smudge of beige eye shadow, blush on my cheekbones and the same clear lip gloss she let Bea wear.

"Mariella isn't part of *our* family," Mom explains to Bea.

Bea shakes her head. "Marry is my sister," she insists.

"Mine too," I can't resist saying, even if there's no use arguing with Mom. It's just that Mariella *is* part of our family. Even if Mom doesn't think so.

"She's your *half* sister," Mom corrects us. "Only whole sisters get to be in this photo. Besides, the photo is for Gramps and Nana. They barely know Mariella."

"What about Sheldon? Why can't he be in the picture? He's my whole cat."

I try not to laugh. Because what if laughing messes up my makeup? But it's hard not to giggle. Whoever heard of a whole cat?

"I hate to tell you this, but that cat isn't exactly whole," Mom says as she reaches into her purse for her fold-up mirror and checks her lipstick.

"Mom!" I say.

"You're right. I shouldn't have said that." Mom clicks the mirror closed. "But in any case, cats don't get invited for family pictures."

Bea points to the big photo on the wall behind me. "Dogs do." I turn to see what she means. In the photo, a middle-aged couple hold hands; there's a Dalmatian lying at their feet.

This time, Mom and I both laugh. Mom strokes Bea's cheek. "You're an awfully clever honeybee!"

I'm about to say I'm awfully clever too when the photographer comes out. She's tall with spiky hair and no makeup. Who needs lip gloss if you *take* the photos?

She says her name is Tara, and she reaches out to shake Mom's hand, then ours too.

When I get up from my seat, Bea does the same. "Could my cat Sheldon be in the photo?" she asks Tara. "He doesn't need lip gloss. But he only has one—"

"Bea," Mom says.

"I don't see why n—" Then Tara catches Mom's eye and stops herself.

"The cat lives at the girls' father's house," Mom explains.

"I see," Tara says. "To be honest, animals are very hard to photograph."

"You did a good job with the Dalmatian," I tell her.

Tara turns to look at the photo of the couple and their dog. "I do like that photo," she says. "But I must've taken a hundred shots before I got it. And bribed Freckles with treats."

"You have treats?" Bea asks as we follow Tara into her studio.

"She means dog treats, honeybee," Mom tells Bea.

One of the things I love about Bea is that she doesn't give up easily. "Maybe Tara has people treats too," she whispers.

The studio is an open area, divided into sections. One has a white L-shaped couch; another has a colorful area rug with baby toys on it; another has a set of folding chairs lined up in a row; and then there's an empty section with navy blue curtains behind it. That's where Tara must have taken the photo of the Russian doll family.

Tara leads us to the couch. Mom says she'd prefer we use the chairs. "I was picturing something traditional—a portrait where I'm sitting and the girls are standing behind me. Maybe they could each have a hand on one of my shoulders," she tells Tara.

Tara purses her lips. Maybe she doesn't like Mom's idea.

"I'd have suggested something a little more casual, less posed. Of course, if that's what you want, we'll do it your way, Lisa."

Mom sits down in the middle chair and adjusts her skirt so it won't have wrinkles. Tara moves the other chairs away. Bea and I go to stand on either side of Mom.

Mom reminds us to stand up straight. Which is kind of funny since she can't even see us. "And Bea," Mom adds, "try not to show your teeth when you smile. You don't want Nana and Gramps to see the spot where your tooth is coming in crooked."

"Darlene says my crooked tooth looks cute," Bea says.

"Honeybee!"

I stand up straight. So far, this isn't exactly fun.

"All right then, ladies, show me some smiles," Tara says. "Not too toothy, Bea!"

Bea raises her hand. "Aren't you supposed to say 'Cheese'?"

When we all laugh, we hear the *click-click-click* of Tara's camera.

"Perfect," Tara says. "Just perfect."

Mom sighs. She loves the word *perfect*. But maybe trying to be perfect is like posing for a photo. Hard work and not exactly fun.

CHAPTER FIVE

We are standing at the arrivals gate at Trudeau Airport.

I've got six balloons (it was my idea to get red and blue and white because those are the colors of the French flag), and Mariella has the cardboard sign that says *Bienvenue Grandmami!* Bea is holding the bouquet of white lilies Dad picked up at the florist. They've got a paper label with Grandmami's name: Lilianne Lamer.

Dad's last name is Lamer too. It's French for "the sea." In Quebec, when women get married, they keep the names they grew up with. That's why Mom kept Tepper. I could use Tepper-Lamer if I wanted, but it's too clunky. Besides, I like having my mom's last name. And even if Dad's French, I've always felt more English.

Mariella speaks three languages: English, French and

Portuguese. Leonor never had a problem with Dad talking to Mariella in French.

Grandmami still lives in the small village in northern France where Dad grew up. Bea has never met Grandmami, since the last time she visited Montreal Bea wasn't even born. I'm excited to see Grandmami again. She's got a crazy sense of humor, and she wears cool clothes. I also can't wait for her to meet Bea.

Dad shifts from one foot to the other. He's wearing his best outfit, and before we left, he polished his tan loafers. They're as shiny as the moon on a clear night.

We know from the arrivals board that Grandmami's plane has landed. But clearing customs takes a while.

Bea loosens the plastic wrap around the bouquet and sniffs the lilies. "How much longer till I meet her?" she wants to know.

"Not much longer," Dad promises.

Mariella and I make a game of matching up the people who come through the arrivals gate with the people waiting for them.

The automatic glass doors open and an old man with a long face and beaky nose steps out. He uses his hand for a visor as he peers out at the crowd.

Mariella nudges me. "That one," she says, raising her eyes

toward a woman with the same beaky nose.

"One point for you," I say to Mariella when the man spots the woman and hurries over to give her a hug. "I bet she's his whol—" I stop myself when I realize how much I sound like my mom. "His sister."

"Mami!" Dad calls out.

"Grandmami!" Mariella and I say at the same time.

For once, Bea is speechless. She watches, her eyes wider than I've ever seen them, as Grandmami rolls two giant suitcases toward us. Grandmami looks more like a French movie star—or a magician—than a grandmother. Last time I saw her she had black hair, but now it's reddish-purple, and she's wearing a red velvet cape.

"Alain," she says, hugging Dad first, then turning to hug Mariella and me. "*Mes petites filles*," she says, which is French for "my granddaughters," as she squeezes us tight. Grandmami smells delicious—like lilac, which happens to be the flower smell I like best. Then she drops to her knees—she's in great shape for an old lady—so she is at eye level with Bea. "Béatrice"—she pronounces Bea's name the French way—"how I have looked forward to this moment." She pronounces *moment* the French way too. Grandmami wipes the corners of her eyes and sniffles in a delicate way. I'm getting a lump in my throat just from watching.

"Grandmami," Bea says solemnly.

"*Que tu es mignonne*," Grandmami says to Bea.

"What does that mean?" Bea asks her.

Grandmami turns to Dad. I can tell from the way her eyebrows shoot up that she's surprised Bea doesn't understand her.

"I speak to the two younger ones mostly in English," he says.

Grandmami pulls her cape over her shoulders. "Ooh la la," she says. "Since French is older than English, and I'm the oldest one in this family, I'll make an effort to speak to the girls *en français*. Girls, here's your first lesson from Grandmami—when you don't know what to say ... *ooh la la* comes in handy. And it has a lovely ring to it."

"Ooh la la," Bea says.

Which makes Grandmami giggle—and wipe her eyes again.

I scoop Bea into my arms. "*Que tu es mignonne* means 'you're super cute,'" I tell her. "Which you are."

Grandmami is going to sleep in my room, and I'll share Bea's room. I'd rather share with Mariella, but Dad said that since she's the oldest and gets the most homework, she needs her own space.

Dad loads Grandmami's suitcases onto a metal cart, and we head for the parking lot.

Bea wriggles out of my arms so she can hold Grandmami's hand. "Those are big suitcases," she says to Grandmami. "Did you bring presents?"

"Béatrice!" Dad says. It's the first time I've ever heard him call her *Béatrice*. He must be doing it for Grandmami.

Grandmami laughs a lot and her laugh sounds more like a girl's than an old person's. "Of course I brought presents for my three *petites-filles*. But it's mostly my own things in those suitcases. I am what you call in English a clothes . . . goat. No, not *goat* . . ."

"Do you mean elephant?" Bea asks.

"Absolutely not an elephant, *chérie*! I'm a clothes, a clothes—"

"Horse!" Mariella and I figure out what Grandmami means at the same time.

"*Exactement*!" Grandmami says. "I still have several big trunks that are being shipped to Canada. They should arrive before the end of the month."

"Big trunks?" Mariella sounds surprised. "Last time you visited you stayed for two weeks. Are you staying longer this time?"

"Elephants have trunks," Bea says.

None of us explain that's not the kind of trunks Grandmami means. That's because Grandmami has stopped in her tracks, put her hand on Dad's shoulder and said to him, "Didn't you tell the girls, Alain?"

Dad brushes his hair away from his face. "I thought we could tell them together." His voice sounds different—less grown-up, more like a kid talking to his mom. Which makes sense, since Grandmami *is* his mom.

We stop walking too. Bea fiddles with the handle of one of Grandmami's suitcases. "Tell us what?" Mariella asks Dad and Grandmami.

Grandmami answers for both of them. "That I am moving in with the four of you. Because to be perfectly *honnête*, I've been worried about my boy."

"For your information, Mami," Dad says, "I'm forty-two years old. Which isn't exactly a boy."

Grandmami pats Dad's cheek. "Forty-two already. Do me a favor, *cheri*, and don't tell too many people—or they'll find me very old."

"You *are* very old," Bea tells Grandmami.

Another grandmother would be insulted. Not ours. She cracks up and quickens her pace to lead the way. She's faster than I expect. Now that she can't hear us, I can tell Dad what's on my mind. "I love Grandmami," I say in a low voice. "But if she's moving in with you, does it mean I'm not getting my room back? And what about the wallpaper? You said you'd tear it off and paint the walls any color I wanted." I hate sounding whiny, but I can't help it. Is it too much to want butter-yellow walls?

Dad reaches out to ruffle my hair. "I know that was the plan, Justine. But sometimes plans change."

I feel bad for Dad. It can't be fun for a grown man to have to live with his mother. But I'm also annoyed. Why does everything in my life have to keep changing all the time? And why do I always have to say yes to it all? Because even if Grandmami is cool—for a grandmother—I'm the one who's giving up my room. And no one thought of warning me in advance. Right now I wish I could have my peeling wallpaper back.

On the way back to Dad's, Grandmami asks Mariella whether she has a boyfriend. "Or a girlfriend," Grandmami adds. "I might be old," she tells Mariella, "but I'm very heep."

"She means *hip*," Dad tells us. "And Mariella's too young for a boyfriend. Or a girlfriend."

"No, I'm not," Mariella says. "But I don't have one."

"I had many when I was your age," Grandmami says.

"*Mami!*" Dad says sharply. Now it sounds like he's the grown-up and she's the kid.

Dad takes the exit toward his neighborhood and drives along Westminster Avenue. The light turns red, and we are stopped in front of Tara Bishop's photo studio.

"Look," I say to Bea, and everyone in the car turns to look.

There, in the middle of the front window, is a giant photograph of me and Bea, with Mom between us.

Mariella whistles. "Hey, you guys are famous!"

I see Dad studying the photo. "It's nice," he says. "Except there's something weird about Bea's smile."

"Mom told me not to show my crooked tooth," Bea says.

"Now why would she say something li—"

Grandmami reaches over to turn on the radio, so we never get to hear the end of Dad's sentence.

CHAPTER SIX

"Fais dodo, Colas mon p'tit frère,

Fais dodo, t'auras du lolo.

Maman est en haut

Qui fait des gâteaux.

Papa est en bas

Qui fait du chocolat . . ."

I'm a terrible singer, but I try hard for Bea. She loves when we sing to her, and it helps her fall asleep. I try to keep my voice soft and low, the way you're supposed to for lullabies. Dad used to sing "Fais dodo" to me when I was little and we all lived together in the country. Thinking about that makes me sad.

Mom only sings English lullabies to Bea, like "Twinkle, Twinkle, Little Star." She won't speak to us in French, though she's perfectly bilingual. I think she's so angry at Dad she's even angry at the language he grew up with.

"Fais dodo" isn't working, and I don't think "Twinkle, Twinkle" would be any better. Bea sits up in her bed. "I'm too happy to sleep. I can't believe I have a grandmami. And that she brought me purple socks." Bea pokes one foot out from under the covers to show me. "How did she even know I love purple?"

"All of France knows you love purple," I tell Bea.

"They do?"

"Of course they do." I run my fingers through Bea's fine blond hair. I want her to fall asleep so she won't be Crab-Bea tomorrow. But also so I can read. Grandmami brought me a French version of Alexandre Dumas's *The Three Musketeers*—it's called *Les Trois Mousquetaires* in French. She said she chose it because Mariella, Bea and I are her *trois mousquetaires.*

No matter how much I love Bea, right now I wish we weren't roommates. If I was in my old room, I'd already be reading. But then I wouldn't have known Bea was having trouble sleeping.

The door is open, so I can hear Dad and Grandmami in the kitchen, speaking in French. I can almost feel my brain working, translating their words. "I'm glad I decided to come," Grandmami is saying. "Though I don't think Justine is happy about giving up her room." When I hear my name I listen extra carefully.

"Justine will come around," Dad says. "She always does."

I can't decide whether or not I like that. Do I really always come around? If I do, maybe it's time to stop. Then again, we can't exactly make Grandmami sleep on the sofa.

I don't want the conversation downstairs to keep Bea awake, so I get up to close the door. Afterward I rock Bea and start singing the lullaby again. "Who's Colas?" she asks. When Bea looks up at me, her blue eyes look so trusting that I feel bad for wishing I was in my old room.

"Colas is the baby brother in the lullaby," I tell her.

"You mean like I'm your baby sister?" Bea asks.

"Exactly."

Bea taps my hip. She does that when she wants something and can't wait. "What about the rest? What does the rest mean?"

I sing the rest. "'*Maman est en haut, qui fait des gâteaux. Papa est en bas, qui fait du chocolat.*' That means Colas's mother is upstairs making cakes. And his dad is downstairs making chocolate."

Bea sighs. "My mom is at the condo," she says. "My dad is in the kitchen with Grandmami." Then Bea thinks of something else. "The mom and dad in the looloo—"

"Lullaby."

"Looloo-bye." Bea can't get it right. But I like *looloo-bye* better than *lullaby* anyhow. "The mom and dad live in the same house?" Bea sounds confused.

"They do." My heart hurts when I tell Bea that. I wonder if I'll always feel sad that our parents don't live together. But I don't want her knowing I'm sad. "'Fais dodo' is a really old looloo-bye," I tell her. "In those days, parents always lived together." Besides, I think to myself, maybe Colas's mom and dad didn't even get along that well. If they did, wouldn't they be making cakes and chocolate in the same room?

Bea is quiet, and I think she's dozing off. But then she says, "Tell me about when Mom and Daddy lived in the same house."

Because Bea was only two when Mom and Dad split up, she doesn't remember when we all still lived together. It's not something I like to talk or even think about. Bea doesn't ask about those days often, but when she does, I try my best to come up with something. Even if it's hard for me. "I remember when you were a baby bump."

Bea giggles. "I was a bump?"

"You were living in Mom's tummy."

"Oh," Bea says. "Tell me more."

"We sang to you when you were in there."

"Did you sing 'Fais dodo'?" Bea asks.

Her question makes me smile. The memory is getting clearer. "No, it was an old song that Mom and Dad loved." The title's coming back to me. "(Everything I Do) I Do It For You." I start to hum it. "We sang it to each other and to you in Mom's tummy. You liked it."

"I did? How did you know?"

"Because you started kicking. Mom pulled up her sweater to show us. We saw your foot moving. Mom said you were clapping."

"Can you clap with your foot?" Bea asks.

I lift one foot and shake it up and down for Bea. "Kind of," I tell her.

Bea giggles. "Are there pictures?" she asks.

"Pictures?"

"From when I was a bump?"

"I'm not sure." As far as I can tell, neither Mom nor Dad keep pictures of the "before" time.

"I wish there were pictures."

"I'll try and find something," I tell Bea. I'm suddenly remembering a scrapbook project I did in grade three. We had to make scrapbooks about our families. With photos and writing. Mom was pregnant in those photos. That scrapbook is at the back of my closet in Mom's condo.

I hear scratching outside Bea's—*our*—room. "It sounds

like Sheldon wants to say good night," I tell her. I'm glad to get a break from so much remembering.

Bea sits up again. "Sheldon!" she says.

When I open the door, the lights are still on in the kitchen. Dad and Grandmami have lowered their voices, so I can't hear what they're saying.

Sheldon jumps onto Bea's bed and makes a circle before curling up at the foot. Bea wants to pick him up, but I explain it's better to let a cat come over when he's ready. "Cats are very independent," I tell her. "Plus Sheldon is still learning to trust us."

"I think Sheldon loves me," Bea says.

"Everyone loves you, Bea. You're extremely lovable."

"I am?"

"Yup. You are. Extremely."

Bea lies back down and closes her eyes. Sheldon is purring at her feet. Soon I'll be able to read.

Dad brought a folding cot up from the basement for me to sleep on. I don't want to wake Bea up, so I stay a little longer on her bed, watching her face and listening to Sheldon's purring and Bea's quiet snore.

When I finally move to the cot, it's super uncomfortable: The mattress is lumpy, and it sags in the middle and smells musty. I don't know how Dad expects me to sleep on it. I'd go downstairs and complain right now, except I don't want to make Grandmami feel guilty for taking my room—and my bed.

It's too dark for reading. If I turn on the overhead light it'll wake Bea up. I have to talk to Dad about getting me a small reading lamp. He worries about money, but maybe we can find one at a garage sale.

I close my eyes and try to imagine myself lying on the soft bed in my off-white room at Mom's condo. The air smells like the lavender mist Mom sprays after she kisses us good night. She says the smell of lavender has been shown to help with restlessness. I don't hear any more talking—or whispering—in the kitchen.

Imagining myself in Mom's condo isn't working.

I can't get comfortable on this lumpy, saggy, smelly cot. I'd feel better if I could read or write. Besides being with my sisters and my friends, reading and writing are the two things that always make me feel better.

But I can't do either of those things in the dark.

I get an idea. What if I write in my head?

Then when I wake up, I can put the words down in my notebook. I can finally feel myself starting to drift off, the words swirling around in my head.

CHAPTER SEVEN

Thursday, Sept. 20

1. Yesterday he was eleven minutes late to get us after school. Luckily one of the pre-K teachers stayed to wait with B.

2. He didn't warn us that GM was moving in, or that I would have to share B's room. These are big changes and he should have told us beforehand—especially me, since I'm the one who lost my room. Kids need time to adjust.

3. He's making me sleep on a folding cot. The mattress is lumpy, it sags in the middle and it smells like mold. Everyone (well, everyone except him!) knows exposure to mold is unhealthy.

4. He said the F-word twice on the way to the airport. He was swearing at another driver. I covered B's ears, but I think I was too late—both times.

5. He drove fifteen kilometers over the speed limit when we were near the airport.

6. He let B skip her bath, even though it was a bath night.

Thank goodness Bea's still asleep. Sheldon hasn't moved from her bed all night. He winks at me with his one eye—and I wink back. He is a very nice cat. Or does a one-eyed cat always seem like it's winking?

I re-read what I just wrote in my notebook to check for mistakes, but I don't find any. I stuff it down to the very bottom of my backpack. I don't want it falling into the wrong hands.

It feels good to start a day with writing. Writing in my notebook almost always makes me feel better.

Downstairs, Mariella is in the living room, talking on her phone. She must have just finished her run because she's in her workout clothes and her face is shiny with sweat. When I hear her say *mae*, which is Portuguese for "mother," I know she's speaking to Leanor. "Okay, I'll tell him Grandmami's invited to the barbecue too. I'll mention the *natas*." When she puts the phone down, Mariella notices me. "You might need to wait to shower at your mom's," she says, high-fiving me.

That's when I spot Grandmami walking down the hallway, clutching a shiny hot-pink cosmetics bag. "*Ne me regardez pas, les filles*," she says, waving us away. "Don't look at me, girls, not until I've fixed my hair."

"Grandmami," Mariella asks. "Can I take a quick shower before you do your hair? I can be done in three minutes, I promise—not a second longer."

"*Eh bien*," Grandmami says. "How can I say no to my eldest granddaughter? To be perfectly *honnête*, I've never been very good at saying no to anyone. Especially your late grandpapa. How I miss that man!"

Grandmami turns to me. "You look so much like your grandpapa—and your papa," she whispers into my ear. I don't want to hurt her feelings by telling her that I wish I didn't. I never met Grandpapa, who died long before I was born. Now I wonder if he had frizzy hair too, and if he's to blame for passing it on to Dad, and then to me.

Grandmami makes coffee while I pack lunches for me and Bea. At least there's whole wheat bread. Dad must've remembered to buy it. If I was interested in recording the *good* things he did, I could write that down, but that's not the point of my notebook. I use it to keep track of all the stuff Dad does wrong—or when he's *negligent*.

Negligent is a word Mom uses a lot when she talks about Dad to Maître Pépin and to Darlene. It doesn't mean Dad is a bad person, only that he doesn't always do the right things when he's looking after us.

Mom is super stressed about our case. She got primary custody of us in the divorce, but now she's asking the court to reduce Dad's access. That means we'd see him less often. Probably just once a week, with no sleepovers. We'd see less of Mariella too, which makes me sad. I could always call her up and make plans. Except making plans to get together with someone isn't nearly as good as waking up in the same house as them.

The thing is, I worry that Mom won't calm down unless she gets her way. What if she stops eating again? I close my eyes and get a picture in my head of how things were two years ago. Mom's at the kitchen table, watching Bea and me eat spaghetti, but there's no plate for her. Mom's eyes look blank, and her cheekbones are jutting out of her face. When I offer her some of my spaghetti, she pushes my hand away. I remember wanting to cry, but knowing I couldn't because that would only make things worse. I open my eyes to make the picture—and those old feelings—disappear.

So even if it might seem mean of me to take notes about all the bad stuff my own dad does, it's my only way to help her.

Once our lunches are packed, I go back upstairs to wake Bea up and make our beds (if you can call my cot a bed). Bea is pulling her T-shirt over her head. I try to help, but she wants to do it by herself. She doesn't say anything about wanting to make her own bed, though.

"*Minhas irmãs.*" Mariella's knocking at our door. *Minhas irmãs* means "my sisters" in Portuguese.

"Hi, Marry." Bea's voice is muffled by her T-shirt.

Mariella's hair is wrapped in a towel. She pats the fold-up cot and wrinkles her nose. "How did you sleep on that stinky old thing?" she asks me.

"So-so."

"Dad said he'd buy you a new bed," Mariella says.

"Dad says a lot of things. He also said he'd get rid of the wallpaper in my old room. I mean Grandmami's room."

Mariella shakes her head. "I know. But he's got a lot on his mind." I don't think I've ever heard Mariella say a bad word about Dad. She's his one-person fan club. Then again, I've never heard Mariella say a bad word about anybody.

"Can you believe Grandmami's moving in? I may never see the inside of the shower here again," I say.

"I feel your pain," Mariella says. "But we have to think about Dad too. It's good for him to have company. Especially on the days when none of us are here. And Grandmami will be paying rent. That'll make things easier for Dad."

"Paying rent? Does Dad need the money that badly?" I say. "And I don't know about Grandmami being good company. Did you notice how annoyed he got when she called him her boy?"

Mariella laughs. "That's just Grandmami being Grandmami. And Dad being Dad. Those two love each other a lot. And you'll get a new bed. I'll make sure of it. Hey, I meant to tell you, you looked amazing in that photo." Mariella pauses. "Your mom let you wear makeup, didn't she? I told you she'd come around one day."

"Yeah," I say, "but it was only for that once."

Mariella is hiding something behind her back. When she takes it out to show me, I think it's a gold pen. She knows how much I love writing.

But it's not a pen. "Mascara," Mariella says, waving me over to the window. She opens the curtain to let in more light. "I need to see what I'm doing."

"What are you doing?" I ask her.

"Isn't it obvious? I'm putting mascara on my *irmãzinha*'s eyelashes. So everyone can see her pretty eyes."

No one ever told me my eyes were pretty. If Mariella's right, I want everyone to see them. On the other hand, I could get in serious trouble for wearing makeup. "Makeup's not allowed at school," I tell her. "Not to mention my mom would disown me if she found out."

"You're forgetting something, *irmãzinha*—I know girls who went to your school. They said the rule was never enforced. Not for a little mascara. Besides, your mom won't see you till four o'clock. The mascara will be worn off by then."

"Are you sure?"

"Am I or am I not the queen of makeup?"

"You are. Your Royal Highness of Mascara—and Lip Gloss."

"Why, thank you, *irmãzinha*. No one's ever called me that before."

Mariella tells me to look up while she applies the mascara. "There," she says, standing back to admire her work once she's done. "Perfect."

When I get to school, my friends notice my makeup right away. Solange claps. "I can't believe you're breaking a rule," she says. I don't admit that Mariella had to talk me into it.

I feel proud when I tell them Mariella put the mascara

on for me. "Wow," Jeannine says. "You're so lucky to have a big sister."

Solange shrugs. "I have a big sister, but she's anti-makeup. For political reasons. She says it caters to the male gaze, whatever that is."

Later, when I wash my hands in the girls' bathroom, I check my reflection in the mirror. Mariella's right. My eyes are kind of nice. I wish I could talk Mom into loosening up the no-makeup rule. But Mom is not the kind of person who loosens up when it comes to rules. Or as she likes to say, "Consistency is the key to successful childrearing."

Consistency is another one of Mom's favorite words, though I sometimes wonder if she uses it to get out of changing things up. What would be so bad about letting me wear mascara—or letting me and Bea have a little more screen time? It's not like screen time would make us blind or reduce our brains to mush.

Consistency isn't the kind of word you'd ever hear Dad use. That's because he's *inconsistent*. He doesn't believe in rules, and if he ever made one, I doubt he'd stick to it.

Dad's inconsistency is another reason why Mom and Maître Pépin think it would be better for me and Bea to spend less time at his house.

When the bell rings, I hurry to my locker. Mom signed a

form giving me permission to pick Bea up after school. It saves Mom time. Probably because I'm rushing, I drop my backpack. Everything spills out onto the floor. My textbooks, my duotangs, my pencil case, my geometry set, even my notebook.

Jeannine picks it up. "Whoa, Justine! Is this a diary? I can't believe you never told us you keep a diary. Did you ever write about me? Did you?" She opens the pink notebook, giggling as she flips through the pages.

"Give it back," I say, grabbing it from her before she can start reading it. "Besides, it's not a diary."

"Then what is it?" Solange asks. "Do you draw in it? I have a book just for drawing superheroes. But I keep it at home."

"It's something I'm doing for my mom," I tell them.

"You mean like a present?" Solange asks.

"Yeah, you could say that. Look," I tell them, "I've got to go. I'm getting Bea."

Mom isn't waiting in her usual parking spot outside Bea's pre-K. But I can see Bea's round face pressed up against the glass front door. She bops when she spots me, and all the stress I felt when Jeannine tried to read my notebook seeps out of me.

I push the door open and Bea tackles me. "Hey, honeybee," I say, picking her up and spinning her in the air the way she loves.

Bea buzzes into my ear, and I buzz back into hers.

Another car is parked in Mom's usual spot. She won't like that.

Now I see Mom's red hatchback coming around the corner. She shakes her head when she notices her spot is taken. I wave and signal that we'll meet her at the stoplight. Mom nods back.

Mom pulls over to pick us up. She gives me a sideways look when we get into the car. "Justine, is it my imagination or does something look different about you?"

I'm about to say it's her imagination when Bea blurts out, "Marry put—" Bea stops speaking when I reach behind my seat and pull on her foot. "Why are you doing that to my foot?"

Mom makes a snorting sound. "What did Mariella do?" she asks. "Justine, let me have a better look at you."

Mariella promised the mascara would be worn off. I put my face so close to Mom's I can see the fine pores on her nose. "There's nothing different about me." My voice cracks. My heart is beating so hard I'm sure Mom can hear it. I never lie to her. I never lie to anybody. I'm a terrible liar.

Mom wrinkles her nose. "You smell different. Did you use a different shampoo at your father's house?"

I'm so relieved I almost laugh out loud. Mariella was right. The makeup must have worn off.

Bea bops up and down in the back seat, excited to know something Mom doesn't. "Maybe it's the moldy smell. Grandmami moved into Dad's house. Justine's sharing my room. And her cot stinks like mold."

Mom puts her hand over her nose. "Mold? Exposure to mold can cause respiratory infection," she says. Then she gives me a sharp look and shakes her head.

She's acting as if smelling like mold is *my* fault.

"Unbelievable," Mom whispers to herself.

CHAPTER EIGHT

Wednesday nights, when Bea and I are with Dad, Mom cooks. She says it's a good distraction. "When you're at his house, and I'm cooking for you, it makes me feel like we're still together," she once told me.

So tonight, like every Thursday, supper is waiting on the middle shelf in Mom's fridge. There's a protein, a vegetable, a carb and always something fruity for dessert, all in rectangular glass containers with snap-on lids. (Mom never uses plastic to store food.)

Bea sets the table while I unpack our dinner. There's roasted tofu, a salad with slivers of carrot and beet, and another container with wild rice. When I unsnap the lid of the tofu container, the smells of ginger and soy sauce fill the kitchen. Though we're not 100 percent vegetarian, we don't eat much meat at Mom's. She says cooking vegetarian food takes more effort, but it's healthier and better for the planet.

I like hamburgers too much to ever be a 100 percent vegetarian. I'm happy Dad still makes them on his barbecue. It's the one time I don't complain about white bread. There's nothing yummier than a burger on an old-fashioned bad-for-you bun.

I'm putting the food in the microwave when Mom comes into the kitchen to see how things are going without her. "I worry you're eating too much meat at your father's," she says. My shoulders tense up whenever she says the word *worry*. Too much worrying makes her anxiety worse. "His idea of cooking is throwing some meat on the barbecue or under the broiler."

My shoulders relax when she mentions Dad's barbecue. Only now I have a serious hamburger craving! Though I'd never tell Mom that, not in a zillion years.

"Sometimes he buys us Chicken McNuggets," Bea tells her. "Chicken McNuggets are delicious. Maybe you could let us have them sometimes."

Mom shakes her head as if she wishes she could unhear what Bea just said. "There's a reason I don't feed you Chicken McNuggets, Beatrice, but I'm not getting into that now."

At supper, Mom sits at the head of the table. Bea and I are on either side, kind of like in our family portrait. Bea and I start eating, but I can't help noticing that Mom is picking at her food with her fork and not actually eating anything.

"Aren't you hungry?" I ask her.

"I had a big lunch," she says. I hope it's true.

When Mom leans in toward me, I think she's about to kiss me, something she wouldn't usually do over dinner. Maybe it makes her feel good that I'm worried about her appetite. But instead she sniffs my hair. "I still smell some mold," she says.

"You do? I showered when I got home. And I washed my hair. Twice."

Bea pops a chunk of roasted tofu into her mouth. "Maybe you should have washed it three times," she says.

Mom wags her finger in the air. "Beatrice, what have I told you about talking with your mouth full?"

Bea swallows the chunk of tofu. "Oops." She moves closer to Mom until her head is in front of Mom's nose. "Do I smell moldy too?"

"No, darling," Mom assures her. "You smell like Bea."

"Phew," Bea says.

I hate smelling like mold. Did my friends notice too? If Solange noticed, she'd have told me. Solange never holds back. It's one of the things I admire about her. She's way braver than me.

I'm going to shower again after supper. But even if I get

rid of the smell, how do I know the mold hasn't already started to poison my insides?

"What did you have for dinner last night?" From the way she asks, you'd think Mom was just making conversation. But I know better. She is looking for more proof that it's bad for us to be at Dad's.

"Dad's spaghetti. I love Dad's spaghetti sauce," Bea says.

Mom wrinkles her nose the way she did when she smelled my hair. "Does he still make it with pork sausage?"

"Yup," Bea says. "Even Grandmami liked it."

"And she's from France," I add. "French people are into food."

"They might be into food," Mom says, "but that doesn't mean they're into healthy eating."

There's homemade applesauce for dessert. Even without any sugar in it, it's delicious. Mom simmers the apples in fresh-squeezed orange juice.

After dinner, Bea and I clear the table so Mom can have some time for herself.

"I couldn't have asked for two better daughters." Mom kisses both our foreheads. Thank goodness she doesn't mention the mold smell again. "Don't forget to scrape the plates before they go into the dishwasher. Food particles jam up the motor, and I want this dishwasher to outlive me."

I'm hoping Mom will take a bath or read a book while we clean up. Instead she goes to use the computer in the den. I bet she's going to research the effects of mold exposure. My nose suddenly feels stuffy. Maybe I'm catching what Mariella had. Or else it's from the mold.

"I'm gonna take another shower!" I call out as I walk past the desk where Mom is sitting.

She doesn't look up from the screen. "Going to," she says. "There's no such word as *gonna*, sweetheart."

"Going to," I say.

Solange says correcting people's grammar can make them feel dumb. It's a habit I must've picked up from Mom. She'd never set out to hurt my feelings; she's just trying to *improve* me. Isn't that what parents are supposed to do—improve their kids? But Solange is right. It makes me feel dumb.

I shut the bathroom door behind me and sniff for mold as I pull my T-shirt over my head. I don't smell any, but Mom's nose works better than mine.

"Justine!" I hear her calling.

"I'm getting into the shower!" I call back.

"I need to talk to you. *Now!*" I tug my T-shirt back on and go see what's up; she's probably just read some terrible fact about cot mold.

Mom is still sitting in the swivel chair in front of the

computer. When she sees me, she shakes her head and starts swiveling back and forth in small half-circles. This doesn't look good.

"The mold's not going to kill me, is it?" I'm careful not to say *gonna*. That could put her over the edge.

"This isn't about the mold, Justine. Although that's one more problem I'll have to deal with. Honestly, I don't think I can take much more."

I get a pit in my stomach when she says that. What happens to a person when they can't take much more? Especially a person like Mom?

Mom's eyes have that shiny look they get when she's about to lose it. "Why don't you read this email I just received from Mrs. Olwen?" Mrs. Olwen is our principal. Why is she emailing my mom?

My body tenses up as I lean over to look at the email.

"Read. It. Out. Loud. Justine." Mom hasn't raised her voice, but I know she's angry from the way she spits out the words. I'd feel better if she went ahead and shouted. Then at least she'd get it out. Holding it in makes Mom's explosions worse.

I'm so used to her being angry with Dad I forgot how bad it feels when she's angry with *me*. Mom's anger is like a wildfire. Once it starts, it quickly gets bigger and bigger. No wonder I feel like I might choke.

"Read. It. Justine."

"I didn't do anything wr—" I start to say, but then my eyes land on the subject line: "Use of cosmetics."

Mariella was wrong. The school must have started enforcing the rule.

Because I don't have a choice, I read Mrs. Olwen's email out loud. I don't cry. If I did, it would make Mom angrier. She doesn't lift her eyes from the screen. It's as if she wants to be sure that I read Every. Single. Word.

> It has come to my attention that today Justine was in violation of our school's rule regarding the use of cosmetics. Please discuss this matter with Justine to ensure that this violation does not occur again. Let her know that should there be a second offense, she will be given one week of after-school detentions.
>
> Yours truly,
> Mrs. E. Olwen

When I am done reading, I gulp from fighting back the tears.

Mom finally stops swiveling. Now she taps her foot on the carpet. "Is this true?" she asks me.

"I guess," I say, because there's no use denying it.

"You guess?"

I can tell from the way she asks that she's running out of patience. "I was wearing eye makeup," I admit.

"I knew something looked different about you when you got into the car." Mom says it like a detective solving a case. "You realize, don't you, Justine, that this kind of thing doesn't reflect well on how I'm raising you, does it?"

"No," I say. It's the right answer. I can't say what I'm thinking, which is, *Why does this have to be about you?* "No, it doesn't."

I could blame Mariella, but I don't. Not only because Mom already dislikes her, but also because I could have said no to Mariella, and I didn't. Maybe a part of me wanted to break the rule—the part of me that is getting tired of *always* following rules. Not just Mrs. Olwen's. Mom's too. Especially Mom's.

CHAPTER NINE

The next morning, because I'm the only one up, I tiptoe to the kitchen. I try not to make any noise as I unscrew the top of Mom's old-fashioned espresso pot.

I've watched her make espresso so often I know exactly what to do. I fill the canister with cold water and spoon three heaping teaspoons of coffee into the metal filter. I try not to spill, and when I spot a few loose grains on the counter, I mop them up with a dishrag. Messes drive Mom crazy. I use the back of the spoon to press down the coffee.

I have a long-ago memory of when Dad used to bring Mom espresso in bed—and how Mom used to say there was no better sound in the world than the *tip-tap* of her husband coming up the stairs with a cup of espresso. Is this the same espresso pot Dad used? I can't ask Mom because she doesn't like talking about the past. She always says, "Don't look backward—you're not going that way."

Bringing Mom coffee in bed is my way of showing her I'm sorry about the makeup. When I tried apologizing last night, she shooed me away. "I'm still too upset to even talk about it," she said.

As soon as I hear the liquid in the pot start to bubble up, I lower the heat. Apparently nothing tastes worse than burned espresso.

When it's ready, I pour the coffee into her favorite mug—the one with a picture of a lioness and her two cubs. Then I put the mug on a saucer and bring it to Mom's room. I use my free hand to knock on the door. She has a no-barging-in-unless-the-condo-is-burning-down rule.

"Mom," I say softly. I hope the smell of espresso will put her in a better mood than she was in last night.

When I hear her say, "Sweetheart," from the other side of the door, every part of me starts to relax—even my ears and toes. Who knew ears and toes could get tense? "Come in. Don't tell me you made espresso? Oh, sweetheart, what a wonderful treat!"

When I walk into her room, Mom is reaching for the pillow on the other side of the bed—the unwrinkled side where no one sleeps. She tucks the extra pillow under her own to prop herself up.

I hand her the espresso. I keep my eyes on her face because I need to figure out if she's really forgiven me. I could apologize again. Or maybe not. What if she's already forgotten about the mascara? Mentioning it might spoil this moment.

Mom takes a sip of espresso. "Mmm," she says. "Perfect."

I can feel my lips curling into a smile. *Perfect.* I am forgiven.

She pats the unwrinkled side of the bed. "Come keep me company," Mom says. "We get so little time just us."

I sit down so I'm facing her. Mom looks at me over the edge of her lioness mug. "I shouldn't have blamed you," she says.

So she's not angry anymore.

But she has something else to say. "Did she put you up to it? Mariella?"

I start to say, "No, she didn't," but Mom talks over me.

"I think Mariella has become a bad influence on you. And I worry that you don't have the strength to stand up to her."

"I'm stronger than you think, Mom," I say. "And Mariella isn't a bad influence. She's a good influence! I love her." My voice cracks. When it does, I don't feel too strong. But what I said just now is true: I'm stronger than Mom thinks. I have to be. "You can't change that," I add.

I'm right. She can't.

Mom doesn't even pretend to listen. "She is a bad influence. You just don't see it. Sometimes I think you're as blind as . . . as . . ." She lifts her hand and when she does, the mug slips off the saucer and coffee spills all over. "Look what you've made me do, Justine. I just bought these sheets, and coffee leaves an awful stain. Go get me the stain remover spray! Now!"

Mom keeps a stack of rags and the stain remover spray at the bottom of the linen closet in the hallway. As I grab the bottle, I can still hear Mom's words in my head. *Look what you've made me do.*

The thing is, I didn't make her do anything.

I didn't make Mom spill the coffee. *She* spilled it.

Mom is tearing the sheets off her bed. I start spraying the stain. It's already starting to fade. I keep spraying. Not just because I want the stain to go away, but also because I'm angry. Angry with Mom for blaming me. Angry with myself for not being able to stand up to her. What's wrong with me anyhow?

"I just washed these sheets two days ago," Mom mutters to herself. Then she notices that I'm still spraying. "Don't use so much spray. It's bad for the fabric." Mom takes the bottle from me.

Bea comes plodding into Mom's bedroom. "Are you two still in a fight?" she asks, rubbing her eyes.

"Of course not," Mom says, without looking up as she gathers the sheets into a pile. "It wasn't a fight. It was a disagreement."

Bea taps my elbow. "Don't fight with Mom. She's bad for fighting with."

Mom looks up from the sheets. "Why would you say that, Beatrice?"

"Because you always win."

Mom laughs as we follow her out of the bedroom. I think for her, always winning is a positive thing. But what Bea said—and Mom's laughter—lightens up the mood in the room.

When Mom speaks, her voice sounds lighter. "Well, I'll say one thing—this coffee stain has lost its fight against me. All right then, girls, it's time for you to get dressed and have breakfast. I need a minute to check my emails and then I have to call Darlene. So just this once, you two can have some extra screen time."

"We can?!" Bea rushes in to hug Mom, who's gone to sit down in front of her computer. "Can me and Justine watch *SpongeBob*?"

"Justine and I," Mom corrects her. "Yes, you and Justine can watch *SpongeBob*. Just don't put the volume on too high. Once I'm done, you can even eat your cereal in front of the TV."

"We can?!" Bea asks again. "What if we get crumbs everywhere?"

"We won't," I tell her. "Cereal doesn't make crumbs."

Mom must not have had much email, because almost immediately she's back in her room talking to Darlene. This would be a good time to check my texts, only I'd need Mom to key in her password if I want to get on the computer—and I don't want to interrupt her conversation.

I sit down in front of the computer. That's when I notice the power light is still on. Mom must have forgotten to shut it down. When I hit the Return key, the screen lights up and opens to Mom's email messages.

I should close the tab. Mom wouldn't want anyone reading her emails. But I'm starting to get fed up with always doing what Mom wants. So before I exit the page, I scan the list of incoming messages. I read from the bottom up. It's mostly work messages, with a couple from Darlene, and another from my nana, and of course the one from Mrs. Olwen.

It's the message at the very top that catches my attention. It's from Maître Pépin. The subject line reads "Re: Curtailment of Visits."

I've never heard the word *curtailment* before. But it sounds serious.

CHAPTER TEN

Grandmami is with Dad when he picks us up. I get the feeling they are discussing something important even before Bea and I get into the SUV. The windows are rolled up, so I can't hear them, but Grandmami is shaking her head and Dad is rubbing his forehead. He does that when he's upset.

When we open the door to get in, we hear Dad telling Grandmami, "How many times have I told you—I need to handle things my way."

Then Grandmami says, "I hate to be the one to tell you, *cheri*, but that's what got you into this in the first place." I don't know which *this* Grandmami means. It's either Dad's work problems, or else the situation between him and my mom.

"*Bonjour, mes petites filles!*" Grandmami says as she reaches into the back seat to give Bea and me each a squeeze.

"You smell delicious," Bea tells Grandmami.

"Thank you, Béatrice," Grandmami tells her. "Today I put on a little Chanel Numéro Cinq. When you girls are old enough, I'll buy you each a bottle."

"Wow," Bea says. "I can't wait to be old and smell so good."

"Is everything okay with you two?" I ask Dad and Grandmami. "You weren't fighting, were you?"

"Of course not," Dad says.

"*Mais non*," Grandmami says at the same time. Which is how I know it isn't true.

Because the sun is shining into the windshield, it looks like there's a halo around Dad and Grandmami. "Mami," Dad says to her, "can you please hand me my sunglasses? They're in the glove box."

Grandmami opens the glove compartment and lets out a little cry. "Alain! *Je ne peux pas le croire*. I can't believe it!" She takes out a packet of cigarettes and waves them in my dad's direction. "You're smoking again!"

"Dad doesn't smoke," I say. "Do you, Dad?"

Dad doesn't answer.

Bea's little body stiffens. "Cigarettes are bad for you," she says. "And so is meat."

"Just give me my glasses, Mami," Dad insists. I think he's angry. It's hard to tell because he doesn't get angry very often. Dad holds his angry in and hardly ever lets it out.

"I won't allow you to smoke," Grandmami tells him. "You know what happened to your father."

"Let it go, Mami," Dad says. "Now isn't the time."

Grandmami bites her lip. "You're still my little boy," she says softly.

What Grandmami said isn't so terrible, but to Dad it must be. Because he does something I would never, ever expect him to do. He turns to Grandmami and says, "*Tais-toi!*"

Tais-toi!?

That's French for "shut up." I've never heard Dad say those words to anyone. Not even to Mom during their worst fights.

Grandmami is also shocked. "Let me out of this truck right now!" she tells him.

Dad slows down. We're on Taschereau Boulevard, which is like a mini-highway. Letting her out here would be elder abuse. Grandmami reaches for the door handle.

"Dad!" I call out.

"I'll let you out," Dad tells Grandmami, "but not here. It's too dangerous."

Grandmami lets go of the door handle. "You know what's dangerous?" she mutters. "Smoking. Smoking is dangerous."

Bea leans over toward me. "Do you think Daddy really smokes?"

Dad turns down a side street, stopping in front of a small

triangle-shaped park. "Voilà," he says to Grandmami. "Here you go."

If I was her, I'd say I'd changed my mind. But Grandmami is as upset with Dad as he is with her. Maybe more. Because when she gets out of the car, she slams the door so hard behind her that the light inside the SUV flickers. I've never seen it do that before.

I'm expecting Dad to go around the block once or twice and then go back for Grandmami—but he doesn't. Instead he pulls into the nearby McDonald's and leads us inside. He tells us to order whatever we want. When I tell him Bea and I shouldn't be eating too much red meat, he rubs his forehead and says, "Look, Justine, I can't handle any more criticism right now."

I explain that I'm just trying to be helpful, and that he should try to eat less red meat too. That's when he pounds his fist on the table so hard that B's tray bounces off. Luckily it was empty.

Mom already warned us that we wouldn't be sleeping over at his house this weekend. That there'll be no more sleeping over until his house gets inspected by a mold expert, and that it's his responsibility to find one. She also warned us not to mention anything about staying over because it might upset him.

Bea orders a hamburger, fries and chocolate milk. He knows we're not supposed to have chocolate milk because it's full of sugar—and that the only kids who should drink chocolate milk are ones who refuse regular milk (Bea isn't one of them).

While Bea is finishing her chocolate milk, she asks him, "Did you find a mold person yet?"

I guess Mom should also have warned us not to mention mold.

Because he gets even more upset after that.

Only this time, he doesn't pound his fist on the table.

This time he starts to cry.

Which is way worse.

ooo

Mom doesn't seem that upset when Bea tells her how Dad said "*tais-toi*" to Grandmami or that Grandmami had to Uber back to Montreal West. Maybe because Mom is upset enough—about the chocolate milk, the cigarettes and that Dad cried in front of us. The crying bothers her most of all. "He shouldn't be carrying on like that around you girls. It isn't right for a man to break down in front of his children."

I decide it's not a good time to say what Solange told me—that her sister thinks the world would be a better place if men started showing their emotions more.

"You know what's really bad?" Bea says to Mom.

Mom sucks in her breath and leans in closer to Bea, which makes me think maybe Mom *wants* to hear more bad news. "Tell me," Mom says. "You know you have to tell me everything, honeybee. That's what moms are for. To tell everything to."

"Well," Bea says, "I was eating a Happy Meal. And I wasn't happy. Not at all."

I stroke Bea's cheek. "Poor bee," I say.

Mom sighs.

"There's something else bad," Bea adds. "I won't get to see Sheldon this weekend."

"And I won't get to see Mar—" I stop myself. The thing is, I really miss my big sister. Texting only makes the missing worse.

Mom claps the way she does when she wants to change the subject. Then she flashes us one of her too-big smiles, which is how I know she's trying to help us forget all the bad stuff that happened when we were with Dad. "Because I'm so glad to have my girls back, I planned something extra special for tonight."

"Is it veggie lasagna?" Bea asks. "I smell veggie lasagna."

Mom tweaks Bea's nose. "You inherited my nose, honeybee. I did make veggie lasagna, and a tossed salad, and fresh fruit for dessert. It'll make up for some of the junk you've been . . ." Mom lets her voice trail off. "I don't want to waste any more time thinking about bad things. Let's think of something fun instead."

"Fun?" I say. *Fun* isn't on Mom's favorite words list.

"That's right. *Fun.*" Mom says it again, like it's an outfit she's trying on, something she wants to like but isn't sure about. "While my two lovees were away today, I didn't just cook. I did some serious thinking. And I reached the conclusion that we need to have more fun together."

Bea's eyes shine like marbles. "Are we going to La Ronde?" La Ronde is the amusement park on Île Sainte-Hélène, which is only a ten-minute drive from Saint-Lambert, where Mom's condo is. Mom hates La Ronde. She says nothing's more depressing than seeing people trying too hard to have fun. Only now it's Mom saying *she* wants to try to have fun!

"Not tonight," Mom tells Bea. "Maybe another time."

Am I hearing things—or did she just say she might take us to La Ronde sometime? "I thought you hated La Ronde," I say.

Either Mom doesn't hear me or she pretends not to. "We have forty-five minutes till the lasagna is ready. And I'm suddenly in the mood for a game of hide-and-seek."

Suddenly in the mood for hide-and-seek? Where did my mom go? Was she kidnapped and replaced by this woman who looks like her and wants to play games?

When Bea covers her eyes, I figure I might as well cover mine too. I count slowly to make it easier for Bea to keep up. "One, two, three, four, five . . ."

I open my eyes a sliver. Mom is tiptoeing down the hallway. Tiptoeing's not her style. She's usually a noisy walker; I think she likes people to know when she's coming. Bea loves when we play hide-and-seek, but Mom has never joined in. Not even once. Even when it's our weekend with her, she's always got grown-up stuff to do, like organizing the condo, paying bills or checking her work emails.

"Sixty-three, sixty-four . . ." Bea stops counting. "Can we open our eyes now? Please!" she shrieks.

"Not until you've counted to one hundred," Mom calls back. Why am I not surprised that Mom wants us to play by the rules?

I hear doors opening and closing, and Mom's footsteps getting farther away. "Eighty-eight, eighty-nine . . ."

Bea stops counting again. "We're almost at a hundred."

"Ninety-two . . . Not quite yet," I tell her. "We have to get all the way to a hundred. Those are the rules."

"You sound like Mom," she says.

"Thanks," I say, though something tells me it wasn't a compliment. But Bea's right. Those words could have come out of Mom's mouth. Am I really that much like her? All my life, I've wanted to be like my mom, but lately, I'm not 100 percent sure anymore.

"We might as well keep counting," I tell Bea. "We're nearly there. Ninety-three, ninety-four, ninety-five . . ."

Bea opens her eyes when we get to a hundred. "Mom!" she shouts. "We're coming to find you!"

Mom doesn't answer. Except for the hum of the air conditioner, the condo is perfectly still. "She's here somewhere, right?" Bea asks, and even if I know there's nothing to worry about, something in my chest tightens.

"Of course she is, honeybee. Mom's playing hide-and-seek with us. C'mon," I say, tugging on Bea's arm the way she usually tugs on mine. "Let's go find her."

Bea bops up and down. "I love hide-and-seek," she says. "I didn't know moms played it. I thought they went to the office and made supper. And worried."

Sometimes Bea seems a lot older than she is.

Bea goes into her room to look for Mom. I hear Bea's giggle as she opens the closet. "Mom? Is that you?"

I head for the den. Mom's not behind the couch. When I check behind one of the overstuffed armchairs, my elbow grazes the shelf with our family photos. One of the frames falls down, hitting the shelf, then clattering to the floor. When I pick it up, I notice the glass is cracked. In the frame is a photo of Mom at the beach with Bea and me. It must be Cape Cod because we used to go there every summer before the divorce. Mom is sitting on a beach towel. She's wearing a straw sunhat and there's sunblock on her nose; she's holding Bea and me close. In the background, there's a sandy beach and blue-green ocean.

I've looked at this photo a hundred times, but it's the first time I ever noticed the jagged line at the top. Someone's been cut out.

It must be Dad. He's not in any of the pictures on the shelf. I take a closer look. Two hot-pink nail-polished fingers are holding on to Mom's shoulder. Mariella. It's Mariella. She used to come with us to Cape Cod. I remember how she and I collected seashells and starfish on the beach while Mom breastfed Bea. I know that Mom hates Dad, but what has she got against Mariella? Mariella never did anything to her.

"Is everything okay?" Mom's voice calls. "Did something fall?"

"Just a picture frame," I call back as I check the carpet for bits of stray glass. I don't find any, but Mom will want to vacuum anyway, just to be on the safe side. I'll do it since I'm the one who broke the glass.

Bea comes running out of her room. She's headed for Mom's bedroom. "You're in here! I heard you!" Bea squeals.

I can hear Bea poking around in Mom's room. I lay the frame on the shelf, with the shattered glass facing up, then I go to Mom's room too.

The door to Mom's walk-in closet is open and I spot the soles of her slippers. She must be sitting at the back of the closet, behind her clothes.

"Mo—" I start to call out, but then I get a better idea. "I'll check Mom's bathroom," I tell Bea. "Why don't you keep looking for her in here? Have you checked the closet, honeybee?"

The sound of Bea's laughter when she finds Mom, mixed with the sound of Mom's laughter at being found . . . well, it's better than the best ice cream or getting an A on an English assignment.

Mom was right.

Of course she's right.

We need to have more fun together.

CHAPTER ELEVEN

The fun's not over! Mom was keeping a surprise from us. When we lived in the Townships, she was into surprises. She organized a surprise tea party for Darlene's thirtieth birthday, and she once celebrated Valentine's Day with me and Dad in the middle of summer. She baked a heart-shaped cake and made us homemade cards.

Tonight's surprise is that Darlene and Will are coming for dinner! Mom said she came up with the plan at the last second. Which isn't Mom's usual style.

Bea and I both love Will, and Darlene too. We don't see them enough because they still live in the Townships, which is a ninety-minute drive east of Montreal. Darlene teaches at a high school there. Maybe that's why she's a bit like a teenager herself. Her hair's gray, but it has one lime-green streak at the front, and her usual outfit is a hoodie with leggings.

Her son, Will, doesn't have a dad. I should say Will doesn't *know* his dad. Everyone *has* a dad. But Darlene had Will on her own. Mom explained it all to me. It was pretty gross. Darlene never met the right man for her, and because she was worried that if she waited too long, she'd never have kids, she used something called a sperm donor. I still don't know exactly how it works. But I once heard Mom tell Darlene she sometimes wishes she'd used a sperm donor too. That it would have been less trouble in the end than being married to Dad. Of course if she'd done that, I wouldn't be me. And personally, I'm glad Dad's my dad.

If I was Will, I'd look at every man I met—especially ones who looked like me, or had my laugh, or were obsessed with computers the way Will is—and wonder, *Are you him?*

Bea and I help Mom prepare for our guests.

I vacuum. It's probably because Darlene and Will are on their way that I start thinking about our old house in the country. It's getting harder for me to remember what living there felt like. I'm glad I'm starting to forget the arguments too, but sometimes I wish I was better at remembering the happy times—the family hikes we took in the woods behind the house, Bea gurgling in the baby carrier on Dad's back; the swimming hole down the road; and the old stone fireplace we'd gather in front of on snowy days, when Darlene and Will would come over and we'd all drink hot chocolate with mini marshmallows on top. Even if the Townships aren't that far away, it feels like our life there happened on another planet in some other galaxy. Maybe I should look for that scrapbook I made back in grade three.

Bea is setting the table.

"Forklift—forks to the left," Mom says. When Mom was little, that was Nana's trick for reminding her where to put the forks. Mom says Nana was very particular—that's where Mom must get it from. "Let's use the linen napkins," Mom adds.

"Dad likes paper napkins," Bea says.

Mom shakes her head. "Of course he does."

"Is that why you got a divorce?" Bea asks. "Because of napkins?"

I'm imagining how funny it would be if a lawyer like Maître Pépin told some judge his client wanted a divorce because of paper napkins. But Mom takes Bea's question seriously. "That isn't why," she says. "Your father and I got divorced because we were too different."

"That's for sure," I say. "And it was about a lot more than napkins."

"We had very different attitudes about childrearing," Mom adds. She often complains about Dad, but she doesn't usually talk about what it was like when they were married and the four of us—five when Mariella was around—were still a family. Maybe our round of hide-and-seek relaxed her. Or maybe it's because she's had a sip of the red wine she opened for Darlene.

"You're a lot stricter with us than Dad is." Mom's not good with criticism, so I'm quick to add, "But that's good. Kids need limits." I've heard her say that two zillion times.

Mom puts down her glass of wine. "I recently read that there are two types of parents, Justine—gardeners and carpenters. Gardeners believe in letting nature take its course." She throws one hand to the left and the other to the right, as if a garden might take root right now in our dining room.

Bea is listening too. "Do they mow the lawn?"

"Rarely," Mom says.

Dad must be a gardener. He lets the grass on his front lawn get super long before he gets around to mowing it. That's definitely letting nature take its course. "What about carpenter parents? What are they like?" I ask Mom.

Mom leans back in her armchair. She'd rather talk about carpenters than gardeners. "Carpenters have plans. They know what they're aiming for. They measure out every plank, then they cut the wood and shape the wood so the pieces fit together . . . perfectly." Her voice lifts when she says *perfectly*.

"You're definitely a carpenter, Mom," I tell her.

Mom picks up her glass of wine from the side table and raises it in the air. "Why, thank you, sweetheart. Here's to carpentry. And to my . . . my"—she is looking for the right word—"my two perfect end tables!"

"Uh, did you just compare us to furniture?" I ask her.

Mom laughs. "I'll admit it doesn't sound right. But it was all I could come up with!"

When the buzzer goes to tell us that Darlene and Will are downstairs, Bea rushes to the intercom—even though she isn't tall enough to reach the button. "Let me do it!" she insists, and Mom lifts her up so she can press the button.

"We're here," Darlene's voice crackles.

"Yay!" Bea shouts.

Mom gives the dining room table a final inspection. She pulls one end of the tablecloth so it's even on both sides. Definitely a carpenter parent.

When they arrive, I can't believe how much taller Will is than the last time we saw him! He's only a year and four days older than me, but he's two heads taller. He's holding a chocolate cake covered in plastic wrap. Yay! Darlene makes the best, chocolatiest chocolate cake ever! It looks like Will has brought something else, in his backpack. Darlene has another bottle of wine and a present wrapped in shiny paper.

She puts down the wine and the present to give Mom a bear hug. "Is it ever good to see you in person!" she says. "All my other friends together don't add up to one Lisa."

Bea tugs on Darlene's arm. "Uh, is that present for me?" she asks.

"Bea!" Mom says. "Where are your manners? Darlene and Will haven't even taken off their jackets. Or tasted our appetizers."

Darlene reaches down to hug Bea. "You're just excited, aren't you, honeybee? It's hard remembering manners when we're excited. The present isn't exactly for you. But I think you'll like it. Why don't you go ahead and open it?"

Bea scoops up the package.

Will has marched into the condo. "I smell lasagna," he announces as he passes the kitchen and the dining room and heads for the den, where the computer is. "So where's the cat?"

"The cat's at our dad's house," I tell him.

"I heard he only has one eye," Will says. "I've never seen a one-eyed cat. Is it totally gross?"

I should introduce Will to Solange. Those two would get along. They both say what's on their minds.

"At first it was a little weird," I tell him. "But then you stop noticing."

"Do you have a picture of him?" Will asks.

Will is just being curious, but his question makes me want to protect Sheldon. "Uh, I'm not sure. What's in your backpack?"

"My Nintendo Switch. What's your Wi-Fi password?" Will takes the console out of his backpack. I'm glad he forgot about Sheldon. Mariella sent me pictures of him, but I don't want Will gawking at him like he's some kind of freak.

"Let me ask you something," I say to Will. "You've known my mom even longer than I have. Do you really think she'd give us the Wi-Fi password?"

Will grins. "Good point. But maybe once the moms start yakking, she'll give it to us—just so we'll leave them alone."

I had forgotten how Will calls our mothers "the moms."

I hear the moms in the kitchen, clinking wineglasses and making a toast. "To best friends—and strong women!" they say together.

Bea comes into the den with the plate of carrots and zucchini Mom sliced up for an appetizer. She is wearing one of Mom's aprons, and I tie the loose strings on the back so Bea won't trip. "Would you like some vegetables?" she asks Will. When Bea smiles up at him, the plate slips out of her hands. Luckily, Will catches it.

"I get extra for that smooth move," Will says, popping two zucchini slices into his mouth.

The moms come into the den. Bea offers them vegetables too.

"You're such a good helper," Darlene tells Bea. "And I love your apron. Even if it's slightly big."

"Does that mean I can open the present?" Bea asks her.

"Of course it does," Darlene says. "I can't believe you waited this long."

Bea starts tearing off the shiny paper. "Try not to tear it, Bea," Mom tells her. "That way we can reuse the paper."

Too late. The wrapping paper is already too shredded to be reused. "It's a cat toy!" Bea squeals. "For Sheldon!" The toy is a black stick with a string at one end, and a fat felt mouse attached to the string.

Mom flashes Darlene a look. "I wish you wouldn't encourage their relationship with that poor cat," I hear Mom whisper.

"Why not?" Darlene mouths the words back to Mom.

Will and Bea are testing out the cat toy. Bea flicks the string, and Will drops to the floor. He's pretending to be a cat, trying to catch the mouse.

Mom and Darlene are still whispering about Sheldon. Mom is worried that having a one-eyed cat will give Bea nightmares. She also thinks Dad got the cat to impress the court—to make the judge think he's some kind of humanitarian. Darlene says that's ridiculous. She thinks having a pet—especially one with only one eye—will make our hearts even bigger than they already are.

Even when Mom and Darlene disagree, it never lasts long. Soon, they are yakking and laughing again. Darlene is telling funny stories about the other teachers at her school, and about the women in her book club who are more interested in discussing recipes than books. Mom rests her feet on the cushion of Darlene's armchair.

Now Bea is pretending to be a cat and Will is flicking the cat toy for her.

"Like I said, I think having a cat is good for them," Darlene tells Mom.

When Mom sighs and says, "Maybe you're right. Maybe I shouldn't worry so much," I'm extra happy Darlene and Will came for supper.

Will winks at me. "Now," he whispers.

"You ask," I whisper back.

Will goes to stand by my mom's chair. He doesn't interrupt the conversation, just waits for an opening.

"Lisa," he says, when Darlene gets up to use the washroom, "can I please have the Wi-Fi password? So I can show Justine and Bea my Switch?" He pauses. "That way, you and Darlene can keep catching up." Though I've known

Will and Darlene my whole life, it still surprises me when he calls his mom by her first name.

"I can't give you the password," Mom says. "But if you give me your console, I'll key it in."

Mom can't see Will giving me a thumbs-up from behind her armchair. She wags her finger at Will. "Don't look," she warns him.

Will turns his head away. Mom keys in the password. I know she's concentrating on tapping the right keys because she doesn't notice when Will turns back. And because he's standing behind her, she doesn't see Will wince.

Mom hands the console back to him and sniffs the air. She takes a long inhale, as if she's already tasting her lasagna. "Dinner's ready! Everyone to the dining room!"

I wonder what Will saw that made him wince.

CHAPTER TWELVE

First Mom wanted to play hide-and-seek. Then she invited Will and Darlene over at the last second. Normally, she'd have planned a dinner with guests a month ahead, and figured out a seating plan—even though there were only five of us!

Now, after supper, when Will suggests we all play *Just Dance*, Mom doesn't automatically say no.

She doesn't say yes either.

But it's a good sign she wants to know what *Just Dance* is. Mom's not into trying new things. That's one way I'd rather *not* take after her.

"It's a party game. I've got it on my Switch," Will tells Mom. "It's better with a dance mat, but Darlene rushed me out, and I left the mat at home."

Darlene doesn't get upset at Will for blaming her. "Can you blame me for being in a rush to see my bestie?" she asks.

"I think Darlene was in a rush for her bestie's lasagna! Anyway, the mat's not big enough for five people," Will says. "I'll hook the game up to your TV and we can follow the moves on the screen. Darlene loves it."

Mom turns to look at Darlene. "Really? You never mentioned *Just Dance* to me." It sounds like Mom's feelings are hurt. Maybe she thinks besties should know everything about each other.

"Probably because we have more important things to discuss," Darlene says.

"That's true," Mom says. "Definitely true."

"*Just Dance* is supposed to be an amazing workout," I say, hoping that'll convince Mom to try it.

"I haven't danced in years," Mom says. "Ala—" She stops herself. "I used to like to dance. But I was never very good. And I don't enjoy things I'm not good at."

"You don't have to be good. You just need to have fun," Will says.

"Fun." Mom repeats the word like she's still getting used to saying it. "I was telling the girls how we need to work on having more fun."

"*Work* on having fun?" Will says. "That's kinda funny."

"Speaking of funny," Mom says, "how about you show us some of those fancy moves?"

I push the armchairs out of the way while Will hooks the Switch up to our TV. Mom and Darlene each take one end of the glass coffee table and drag it over to the window.

"Let's show them how we do 'The Final Countdown,'" Darlene suggests.

"Oh my God," Mom says. "I remember dancing to that in the eighties. Where did the time go, Dar?"

"Someone turn out the lights," Will says.

Bea stands on one of the armchairs and tries to reach the switch. "Bea!" Mom says. "Get down from there! You could hurt yourself! Besides, those chairs aren't made for standing on."

I help Bea down from the chair, then I turn off the lights.

The music is so loud it makes the whole room pulse. On the TV screen, a colorful character moves to the beat. Darlene and Will are in front of the TV, following the figure's moves—or at least trying to. They clap when he claps and swivel their hips when he does. There is a one- or two-second time lag, but you can tell they've had a lot of practice. I can just picture the two of them boogying in their living room in the Townships. Bea joins in, then I do too.

At first, Mom watches from the side of the room, then she throws up her arms and starts dancing. I'm so used to her being an adult that it feels weird—in a good way—to see her act more like a kid.

Will has to turn up the volume twice because we're all laughing so hard.

The next song is Beyoncé's "Single Ladies." "This song is made for us, girls!" Darlene shouts over the music. "Single ladies rule!"

"Not Will. Will's not a lady," Bea says.

"I'm a single boy!" Will shouts. "Single boys rule too!"

When the character kicks out his left leg, we kick ours out too. Because the den is dark, I don't see how close Will is and I end up kicking his butt. "Ow!" he shouts, rubbing the spot where I kicked him.

"Girls kick butt!" Darlene shouts.

Mom and I laugh so hard we miss the next two moves.

"Swivel those hips," Darlene tells us. "Now kick and cross your hands over your heart."

"I can't watch the screen and listen to you at the same time," Mom tells her.

Will, Bea and I sing along as we swivel and kick and cross our hands over our hearts.

Mom slaps her thigh even though it isn't part of the moves.

Darlene reaches out for a high-five when they get to the part in the song about putting a ring on it.

"We don't need rings, girlfriend!" Mom shouts, high-fiving Darlene back.

A half-hour later, Mom and Darlene are winded from so much dancing. Bea can hardly stand.

"Justine and Will," Mom says, "could you two put Bea to bed? That'd give Darlene and me a little more grown-up time before she and Will head home."

Bea is too tired for a story. She's even too tired to tell Will about Sheldon. "You need to brush your teeth and floss," I say as I lead her down the hall.

"Can't she skip that for once?" Will asks.

"You're supposed to brush and floss every single night," I tell him. "Unless you want your teeth to fall out."

"Says who?" Will asks.

"Says the dentist. And my mom."

"*My mom*," Will says, making it sound like I'm part of some cult that worships mothers. "Do you always do what she says?" he asks.

I pause for a second before I answer Will's question. "Yeah. I guess I do. Or at least I try to. Are you saying listening to my mom is a bad thing? She happens to be very smart."

"I'm not saying she isn't."

"What are you saying, then?"

"I'm saying we're old enough to think for ourselves. To

have our own opinions. The way I see it, your mom's bitter. And she's dragging you into her mess."

I can't believe what Will just said! "Bitter? My mom's not bitter, and she's not dragging me into anything. And for your information, I have my own opinions!" Only once I've said that, I'm not so sure it's true. Could Will be right? Is my mom dragging me into her mess? Is she bitter? No, no way! For one thing, Mom doesn't make messes. She's just overwhelmed. And even if she'd never ask me, I know she needs my help. Besides Darlene, who else has my mom got to help her?

I don't know what else to say to Will, so I scoop Bea up and bring her to our bathroom. I set her down on the pink plastic stool in front of the sink. "Time to brush and floss," I say, using my fingers to comb the hair out of her eyes. "You've got to. Even if you're tired, honeybee." I glare at Will's reflection in the mirror. What makes him think he has the right to criticize me—or my mom?

"Can you two stay with me till I fall asleep?" Bea asks us once we've brought her to her room and I've bundled her into bed. "But no fighting." I'd thought Bea was too tired to pay attention to my conversation with Will. But Bea is always paying attention, even when I think she isn't.

She rests her head on her pillow, then reaches out her hands so Will and I can each hold one. Bea closes her eyes.

"My cat's name is Sheldon," she says as she begins to doze off.

I can hear the quiet murmurs of Mom and Darlene in the kitchen. I don't want to stay angry with Will. He's my oldest friend. "I wonder what they're talking about," I say to him.

"Your dad," Will says. "They're always talking about your dad."

"No, they aren't," I say. "They talk about us too. And they talk about what it was like when we were neighbors. And your mom talks about her school and book club friends."

"Your dad's still their favorite subject. Your mom's pissed about the mold at his house. I heard her say your hair stunk even after three showers."

I can't help sniffing the air. Could my hair still stink? If it does, how will I ever get rid of the smell?

"Your mom told my mom that the mold situation could help her legal case. But not enough. She needs more scoop."

"Scoop?"

"Yeah, you know, *scoop*. Evidence to prove he's a bad father."

"He's not that bad," I tell Will.

"Your mom thinks he is," Will says. "And you know how my mom operates. Unless something totally ticks her off, she mostly goes along with whatever your mom says. It's the secret to their long and happy friendship."

"How do you know my mom thinks my dad is bad?"

Will doesn't answer straightaway. He's deciding whether or not to tell me something. He opens his mouth to speak, then shuts it.

"How do you know?" I prod him.

"The Wi-Fi password," Will says.

"What's the password?"

"AWFULALAIN. All uppercase," Will says. "Should you ever need it."

CHAPTER THIRTEEN

It's Saturday morning and Dad is waiting in the driveway in front of the condo. He doesn't open the back of his SUV the way he usually does so we can toss in our backpacks. Bea and I didn't pack anything, since we won't be sleeping over until he finds a mold expert who can give his house the all-clear.

"You know your father," Mom said when she walked us to the elevator. "It could take weeks. Possibly months. Organization was never his strong suit."

Sheldon is sitting in his cat carrier on the back seat. Bea squeals when she sees him. Sheldon pricks up his ears, then starts to purr. Bea purrs back.

"I didn't know you spoke Cat," I tell Bea. "You really are gifted."

"I must speak Cat too," Dad says, "because when I told Sheldon I was going to pick you two up, he told me he was coming." He pauses, then calls out, "Seat belts!" while meeting my eye in the rearview mirror. "I'm trying to impress you here, Officer!" he says with a grin.

I'm always a little startled when I look into Dad's eyes. Probably because they're so much like mine.

"Don't forget Sheldon's seat belt," Bea says after I check that she's buckled in to her car seat. I fasten the middle seat belt around the cat carrier. Bea nods her approval. "How's Grandmami?" she asks Dad. "Did you two make up?"

"She's fine. And yeah, we made up. She's a good person—and she does keep me laughing," Dad says.

"Did you say you were sorry for telling her to shut up?" I ask him.

"I did," Dad says to the windshield. "It wasn't right of me. And I owe you two an apology too. I'm sorry."

"We've heard worse," Bea says.

Dad chuckles. "Where exactly have you heard worse?" he asks Bea.

"At pre-K," Bea says. "It's mostly the boys. But some of the girls say bad words too." She opens the small hatch at the top of the cat carrier. Now there's just enough room for Sheldon to poke his head out. Bea leans over to give him a nuzzle. "Mom says it could be a long, long time before we get to fall asleep together," she tells him.

Dad tightens his grip on the steering wheel. "Now why would your mom say something like that?"

I answer before Bea can. Because you never know what Bea might blurt out. "Mom thinks it could be hard to find a mold expert," I say.

"Mom says organ . . . organi . . ."—Bea gives up on the word—"is not your pants or jacket."

"Pants or jacket? What are you talking about, Bea?" Dad looks at me in the rearview mirror again. "Justine, do you have any idea what your sister is talking about?"

"Pants or jacket?" I'm stumped too. Then I get it. "Mom said organization isn't your *strong suit*." I crack up. That has to be one of Bea's funniest mistakes ever.

Dad doesn't think it's funny.

I'm half expecting him to say something mean about Mom, but I'm starting to notice Dad *never* says anything mean about anybody. When it comes to Mom, he mostly avoids mentioning her altogether. It's one more way in which my parents are different.

"Not my strong suit." Dad makes a harrumphing sound. "For your information, I have plenty of pants and jackets. And by the way, I found a mold expert. He's coming first thing Monday."

"You found him?" Bea says. "Did you hear that, Sheldon?"

"To be honest," Dad says, "I didn't find him myself. Your grandmami did. Organization is definitely her pants and jacket."

When we get to Dad's, he sets the cat carrier down in the front hall.

"Come see what we're up to!" Grandmami calls from the kitchen. Bea and I hurry inside. Mariella and Grandmami are at the kitchen table, doing a puzzle. From what I can tell, Dad's apology worked—or else he and Grandmami have declared a truce.

"I like puzzles," Bea says. "Especially hard ones."

Mariella pats the seat cushion on the chair next to hers. I sit down. Bea takes the spot across from me. Now we can work on the puzzle too.

"Grandmami brought it from France. It has a thousand pieces," Mariella tells us.

"A thousand is a lot," Bea says.

Mariella sneezes. How can she already have another cold? I better remember to wash my hands later, and to remind Bea to wash hers too. Simple hand washing is the best way to prevent the spread of germs.

Grandmami shows us the picture on the puzzle box. It's a beautiful old gray building overlooking a rocky coast and the navy-blue ocean. "It's an abbey on the Atlantic

Ocean in Normandy, in the town where I grew up and your father was born. I went to services so many Sundays at that abbey my picture should be in this puzzle! One day, I'll take you three girls there." Grandmami wipes the corners of her eyes. Maybe she didn't really want to move here. Maybe Mariella is right and Grandmami did it for Dad. Even if the hair near Dad's temples is getting gray and he doesn't like when she calls him her little boy, she's still his mother.

Dad wants to know if we want hot dogs for lunch.

I look up from the puzzle. "Hot dogs contain nitrites," I tell him.

At first I think he isn't listening. He's taking the hot dogs out of the fridge and there's a bottle of ketchup on the counter. I think about my notebook, which I left at Mom's condo, safely stashed at the bottom of my backpack. *D fed us hot dogs full of nitrites, and also ketchup, which everyone knows is one-quarter sugar.*

"Come here, will ya, Justine? Lemme show you something." I don't want to make Dad feel dumb, so I don't tell him *lemme* is not a real word.

"See this?" he says, when I go over to where he is standing by the sink. Dad points to the nutritional label on the hot dog package: *Nitrite-free.* "I bought these hot dogs at the *health food store*," he says. I'm waiting for him to add that he did that so I wouldn't give him a hard time.

But he doesn't say that.

"I bought them because I love you."

I swallow. I know from the way he's looking at me that Dad wants me to say I love him back. And though I do love him—what kid doesn't love her own father?—the words get stuck in my throat. I don't know why. They just do.

I reach for the ketchup. Dad watches me, a half smile on his face. "One hundred percent organic. Picked it up at the health food store too," he says.

Part of me is happy Dad made a special trip to buy nitrite-free hot dogs and healthy ketchup. But this other part of me is a bit, well . . . disappointed. Now what will I have to write about in my notebook?

Then another thought comes to me: Dad is Dad. He will always be Dad. Which means that before we go back to Mom's condo, I'll have lots more material to report on.

"Look!" Mariella calls out. "I found a piece that fits." It's a bit of a surprise to me that someone who's fifteen still likes doing puzzles. Maybe it's because she's happy to be hanging out with Grandmami—and us, of course. Mariella is working on a tower on the far side of the abbey. "Bea, can you look for pieces with small gray stones?"

Bea is jamming random puzzle pieces together. She sighs at Mariella's request. "Gray is boring. Too bad it's not a purple castle."

"There aren't any purple castles in France, honeybee," I tell her. "But how about I help you find the gray pieces?"

"Is it true you two aren't sleeping over?" Mariella asks me.

"My mom's worried about the mold," I tell her.

Grandmami nods. "*Ta mère s'inquiète toujours*," she says.

Bea stops looking for puzzle pieces. "What does that mean?" she asks.

Mariella translates. "Grandmami said, 'Your mother worries all the time.'"

Bea goes back to looking for the puzzle pieces Mariella wants. "Our mom worries all the time," she says to herself. "Well, maybe not *all* the time. But most of it."

CHAPTER FOURTEEN

Nitrite-free hot dogs and organic ketchup don't have much flavor. The hot dogs Dad usually makes taste more hot-doggy. And I like their sweet, smoky taste. That's what I'm thinking when someone knocks at the front door. There's a doorbell, but it's broken and—surprise, surprise—Dad hasn't gotten around to fixing it.

"I'd better see who that is. I really need to fix the darned bell," he mutters. "I better put it on my to-do list."

Dad's kitchen table was our dining room table in the Townships. Mom let him keep all the furniture from the old house. She said she wanted the condo to have a "contemporary feel." Which means new. Actually, Dad didn't exactly *keep* the furniture. He paid Mom for it. It was part of the divorce settlement. I remember finding a sheet of paper on our old kitchen counter. Mom had listed every piece of furniture and how much it was worth. Even the kitchen curtains were on the list. For some reason I still remember the price. One hundred and forty-five dollars. Which seemed like a lot of money for plain white curtains.

Mom wanted a fresh start. That's also why she wanted to move to the South Shore of Montreal—even if it meant more driving for Dad. "Not that I'm going to give him the furniture for nothing," I'd heard Mom tell Darlene. "That man owes me after what he put me through." I don't know what it was exactly that Dad put Mom through, but I figure it had to do with his business tanking and Mom having to suddenly be on a budget and go back to working full-time.

I wonder if when Dad sees the kitchen table, the one-hundred-and-forty-five-dollar curtains, the plaid couch in the living room and his bedroom furniture, he thinks about the past. And if he does, whether it makes him sad or lonely. But those aren't the sorts of questions I'd feel comfortable asking him.

"There's ketchup on the side of your mouth," I tell Dad as he gets up to answer the door. I point to my own face to show him where the ketchup is.

Dad licks it off. At least it isn't shaving cream. "What would I do without you, Justine?" he asks.

"We forgot to let Sheldon out of his cat carrier!" Bea

calls out, but Dad is already halfway to the front door. He's marching and humming "La Marseillaise," the French national anthem, which is why he doesn't hear.

"Mami!" Dad shouts from the vestibule. "Good news! Your trunks are here!"

"*Non*," Grandmami says. "*Impossible!* They're not supposed to arrive before next week!" But she gets up from the table just the same, and goes to the living room so she can look out the front window. She presses her face to the glass the way Bea does at pre-K. "*Merveilleux!*" Grandmami gushes. "It really is my trunks!"

Dad has gone out to the front porch, leaving the front door wide open. I can hear one of the delivery people saying there's a paper for him to sign.

Bea kneels down by the cat carrier and opens up the wire latch. "Sorry, Sheldon. We got busy with a puzzle, then we had hot dogs. Healthy ones."

Sheldon pokes his head out of the hatch and looks around—first toward the inside of the house, then out at the porch and the street.

"You want to go outside, don't you?" Bea says.

"He's an indoor cat," I remind her. "He's not supposed to go outside." But it's too late. I hear a loud meow, and I see a flash of fluffy gray tail. Then nothing.

"He wanted to go outside," Bea is saying.

I rush to the front porch. Bea follows close behind me. Dad is directing the delivery people as they carry the first trunk up the steps. "Did you see a gray cat?" I ask them.

They shake their heads.

Dad wipes his forehead. "The cat got out?" he says. "Let me help them get this trunk inside, then I'll go find him."

"Mariella, *viens m'aider*, come help me," I can hear Grandmami saying from inside. "We need to move this desk to make room for my trunks."

"Sheldon!" Bea's voice is so high that for a second, everyone stops what they are doing. Even the delivery people put the trunk down on Dad's front steps.

What happens next happens very quickly.

Bea runs past Dad, then down the front steps, past Grandmami's giant trunk. She's barefoot and moving so quickly her pigtails look like they're taking off from the back of her head. Dad calls out, "Bea, get back here now!" But it's as if Bea can't hear him. *Won't* hear him.

One of the delivery people had leaned over and tried to block Bea's way, but she was just nimble enough to dodge around him.

"Sheldon! Sheldon!" Bea screams.

She's headed for the street.

Dad takes off after her. And I take off after him. Grandmami and Mariella have come to the front porch. "Bea! Stay on the sidewalk!" Mariella calls out.

I see Bea's small body up ahead. She lifts one hand in the air, as if she's trying to wave. Has she spotted Sheldon? That's when I see another flash of gray. Sheldon is sitting on the sidewalk across the street.

"Get back here now!" I hear Bea call out to Sheldon. The same words Dad used a few seconds ago. Then Bea does something she knows she's not allowed to—she crosses the street. Running. Automatically, I do what Bea hasn't done: I look both ways. Thank goodness Dad lives on a quiet street, and there's no oncoming traffic.

"BEA! STOP! NOW!"

I've never heard Dad raise his voice before. I didn't even know he could raise his voice. The sound is so loud my eardrums hurt.

Dad runs over to where Bea is. Then he swoops down like some giant bird and grabs her by her shoulder. He turns her head so he can look straight into her eyes. Their faces are practically touching. "HOW MANY TIMES HAVE I TOLD YOU NEVER TO CROSS THE STREET BY YOURSELF?" he shouts.

Bea is shaking and whimpering.

Dad picks her up and tucks her under his arm.

Sheldon hasn't moved from his spot on the sidewalk. With his one good eye, he is watching the commotion he has caused.

Dad uses his free hand to grab Sheldon. Sheldon lets out another noisy meow. But he doesn't scratch Dad or try to get away. He must realize that Dad means business.

Dad's panting, and his face is pale and sweaty when he marches past me and back toward the house, Bea in one arm and Sheldon in the other. I follow behind him as he squeezes past Grandmami's trunks, marches inside and tosses Sheldon into the living room. Sheldon lands on the carpet with a thump, then goes to hide under the plaid couch. He doesn't seem to realize that his tail is still sticking out.

Dad doesn't say a word. Maybe he's still too angry, or maybe he has to catch his breath.

That's when I hear Bea say, "You scared me, Daddy."

Dad takes a long, noisy exhale. "You scared *me*, Bea," he tells her, setting her down on the floor. "You scared all of us."

"But you shouted," Bea says. "You never shout."

"I shouted because I was scared," Dad tells her. "And angry. How many times have I told you never to cross the street—any street—by yourself?"

Bea drops her head. "A lot of times. But I forgot," she whispers.

Now Bea starts to cry. At first I think it's because she feels bad for not having looked both ways. But it isn't that. "Ow, Daddy," she says. "You hurt me."

He hurt her? What's she talking about?

"Ow," Bea says again. "My shoulder."

Now I remember how Dad grabbed her shoulder before. He didn't mean to hurt her.

"Do you want me to get a Band-Aid for your boo-boo?" I ask Bea.

"Yes, please," she answers. Then she starts crying even harder. When Dad puts his arms around her, she pushes him away.

I'm on my way upstairs to get the Band-Aid box when I hear Bea say, "I want my momma."

That's what gives me the idea. Bea wants Mom. And Mom wants us.

I think about how much Mom wants to win her case and about how stressed out she's been. Then I remember what Will said about Mom needing more scoop.

This could be the scoop Mom needs. I wouldn't be lying. I'd just leave out some of the story.

Once I get back to Bea, I pull the neck of her T-shirt over so I can see her shoulder. It's red, but the skin isn't broken. She doesn't need Band-Aids. But they'll make her feel better.

I arrange three Band-Aids on Bea's shoulder—enough to cover the whole area. "This'll help the boo-boo," I tell her.

I'm talking to her, but in my head I'm someplace else. Back in my memory, selecting the details. The details that will help Mom. Because I'm the only one who can.

The way the neck of Bea's T-shirt is all stretched out.

The way she said, "You scared me, Daddy," and "Ow, Daddy, you hurt me."

The tears rolling down her cheeks, leaving wet tracks.

The way she pushed Dad away and said, "I want my momma."

The three Band-Aids.

I can use all of it in my notebook.

CHAPTER FIFTEEN

I wish my notebook wasn't at Mom's. So I grab a piece of scrap paper and start writing. I can copy my notes over later, when we're back at the condo.

Saturday, Sept. 29

He went crazy.

I've never heard anyone shout so loud.

And he hurt B's arm.

She said she's afraid of him.

How will she ever be able to trust him again?

And how do we know he won't do it again?
Next time could be worse.

He got upset.

First he shouted, then he grabbed B by the shoulder. The neck of her T-shirt is all stretched out. (I had to use three regular-size Band-Aids to cover the sore spot.)

I'm going to need Bea's help if this is going to work, and we don't have much time.

I need to make this happen before we see Mom, and I can't talk to Bea while Dad's around.

That leaves me just the time between when he drops us off in front of the condo and when Mom meets us in the lobby. I need to work fast.

But Mom isn't in the lobby. Usually, she's standing by the inside doors, then once she spots Dad's truck, she backs away. Where is she?

"That's weird," Dad says, more to himself than to us. "I'd better text her."

"Maybe not," I say. He doesn't know that Mom wanted to block his number so he wouldn't be able to text her *ever*, except Darlene told her that would be totally irresponsible. "What if he needs to reach you about something to do with the girls?" Darlene pointed out. "You may not want to hear this, Lisa. But one of these days you're going to need to learn to get along with Alain again. For the girls' sake.

There are plenty of people out there who get along with their exes. And some of those exes have done worse things than go broke." So Mom didn't end up blocking his number, but her face tenses up and she chews on her lip anytime he texts.

"She needs to buzz you in and I'm not leaving you two here unattended," Dad says without looking up at me. I take a deep breath and exhale slowly. This is going to take a while. Dad holds the record for slowest texter on the planet. He uses one finger and, because his fingers are stubby, he makes tons of mistakes—then he wants to correct them, which makes him even slower.

I watch Dad tap on the keys with his middle finger, then groan when he finds a mistake and tries correcting it. He taps harder, as if he thinks that will help.

"Why don't you just let me do it?" I say.

When he answers, "No, I got this," he reminds me of Bea wanting to put on her overalls by herself. When Dad finally presses Send, he turns to Bea and me. "I told you I could do it," he says. Then he swivels in his seat, reaches for Bea's hand and rubs the top of it. "How's that boo-boo of yours?"

"It still hurts," Bea says. "Justine put on three Band-Aids. Three's a lot of Band-Aids."

"Look, honeybee," Dad tells her, "I'm sorry about your

shoulder. And I shouldn't have forgotten Sheldon in his cat carrier."

Bea gulps. "I'm glad Sheldon's okay," she says.

Dad turns fully around so he can look into Bea's eyes. "I need you to promise you'll never, ever cross the street alone again."

Bea swallows before speaking. "I promise."

Dad nods. "All right, then. And I'm going to need to tell your mom about what happened."

"I can do that," I offer. For my plan to work, I need to be the one to explain things to Mom.

"Better leave it to me," Dad says. His phone pings. Mom is texting him back. I watch as his eyes move across the tiny screen. He doesn't look upset, so she must be okay.

Dad slides his phone back into his pocket. "She's got a migraine."

"She does?" I say. That's a bad sign. After she and Dad split up, Mom got a lot of migraines. Some days, her head hurt so much she couldn't leave the bed. But she hasn't had one for ages.

"She says that once she buzzes you up, you should let yourselves into the apartment. She wants you to brush your teeth and put yourselves to bed. Sheesh, you two, you'd have been better off staying at my place tonight," Dad says.

"You have mold," Bea reminds him.

"I don't have mold." Dad sounds annoyed.

"Don't tell Mom what happened. Not when she has a migraine."

"You're right," Dad says. "I'll tell her tomorrow."

"You'll come for us tomorrow morning?" I ask him.

"Absolutely." He gets out of the car to hug us goodbye. He's careful not to touch Bea's shoulder. The engine is still running.

"Idling is a bad habit," I remind him. I got that slogan off a bumper sticker and I've never forgotten it.

Dad ruffles my hair. "When I grow up," he says, "I want to be you, Justine."

It's a joke. But maybe Dad doesn't like being reminded of what to do all the time. Maybe reminding people of stuff is like correcting their grammar. Maybe it makes them feel dumb.

Then again, if Dad remembered to turn off the motor, and to tell us to buckle up, I wouldn't have to bug him all the time. There's another thing Mom says a lot: "That man will never grow up." (Even though I once heard her tell Darlene that when she first met Dad, she liked that he was playful.)

Dad is pretty much admitting Mom's right. He still hasn't grown up. No wonder that sometimes when I'm around him, I feel like *I'm* the adult.

"If he doesn't have mold," Bea says to me as we walk into the lobby, "why can't we sleep over?"

"Because he *might* have mold. You know Mom—she's very protective," I tell her. I pick her up so she can press the code for Mom's condo. Bea's getting heavier for me to lift. My little sister is growing up. It makes me happy and sad at the same time. "You're getting bigger, honeybee. Soon you're gonna be able to reach all the way up without me. I mean, *going to* be able to reach."

"Really?" Bea sounds surprised. The buzzer sounds and I yank open the lobby door.

"Really. Bea, there's something I need to talk to you about. Something important," I say to her as we head to the bank of elevators.

Bea nods solemnly.

I look into her eyes the way Dad did before. I need to make sure I have her full attention. "You know how much you love Sheldon?"

Bea pauses to think about the question, then she opens her arms as wide as they'll go. "I love Sheldon this much. Even more."

"That's right. That's why you have to promise me you won't tell Mom—or anyone else—what Sheldon did."

I can see from Bea's eyes she's confused. "Why not?"

"Because Mom will blame Sheldon for what happened." I pause because I really need what I'm about to say to sink in. "And then she'll make Dad get rid of him."

I'm glad Bea doesn't ask what "get rid of him" means. Instead, she says, "No," in a tiny voice. I can tell she is trying not to cry. Maybe she is all cried out from before.

"When Mom hears about your boo-boo, she's going to ask you what happened. You can't say Sheldon ran off, or that Dad grabbed you when you took off after Sheldon. And you definitely can't say you crossed the street alone."

When Bea nods slowly, I think maybe that's all I need to say. Bea's got the point. But then she thinks of a question. "What do I tell Mom?"

I don't stop looking into her eyes. When she looks back at me, I know she understands how important this is. "Tell her Daddy hurt your shoulder. And you're scared of him."

"Okay," Bea says, nodding slowly. "I won't tell the part about Sheldon. Or that I crossed the street alone."

"Mom will want to know why Dad got so upset." To be honest, I'm still figuring this next part out myself.

But Bea figures it out for me. "I'll say Daddy got upset for no reason."

Now I'm the one who nods. I wouldn't have thought of that. But it works. Sometimes people get upset out of nowhere.

Though she'd never say so flat-out, Mom needs my help. The headaches happen when she has too much to handle. Her job, looking after us, worrying when we're at Dad's. Last time it started with the headaches, then the staying in bed, then the not-eating. Then the doctor's diagnosis and the pills she stopped taking.

What Bea just came up with . . . that's *scoop*.

CHAPTER SIXTEEN

When Bea and I go into the kitchen on Sunday morning, the lights are out. Mom is sitting in her usual spot, her palm pressed against her forehead. She's not making a grocery list or looking for healthy recipes the way she usually does on Sunday mornings. She's just sitting.

"Let's not be too loud," I whisper to Bea. "Mom's head still hurts."

Mom looks up at the two of us. She smiles, then bites her lip. Smiling must make the headache worse. I notice fine lines I've never seen before at the outsides of her eyes.

Bea runs to the table. "Look at my boo-boo." Then she remembers to drop her voice. "Daddy did it," she whispers. "For no reason." She meets my eyes when she says that, and for a second I feel bad for her.

But then I remind myself that what I told Bea is true: If Mom knew the whole story, she'd make Dad get rid of Sheldon.

I go stand next to Bea, take her small, warm hand in mine and squeeze it. It's my way of telling her she's being a very good girl.

"Oh my God," Mom says, and her face, which is already pale, turns gray. I hate to upset her, especially when she has a headache, but I remind myself that everything I'm doing, everything Bea is doing—even if she doesn't realize it—is all to help Mom.

"For no reason?" Mom's voice sounds a little stronger. She turns to me. "Justine, is that true?"

I take one deep breath. Then I nod.

This next part is very important.

"For no reason," I say, repeating Bea's words. Then I add something else. "I think he's starting to lose it."

When I say those words, I have the weirdest feeling that I'm actually telling the truth. That I'm starting to believe my version of what happened.

Besides, it isn't a total lie. We just left some stuff out. Everyone knows that isn't the same as lying.

I squeeze Bea's hand again, and this time, she squeezes mine back. She needs to understand we are in this together.

Mom gives her head a shake as if that will help her headache go away. “I knew it,” she whispers.

“Justine put three Band-Aids on,” Bea says. “And they were the jumbos.”

Mom lifts Bea onto her lap. Then, very gently, she pulls down the corner of Bea’s pajama top so she can check Bea’s shoulder. The area around the Band-Aids has gone from red to pink. “My poor sweet honeybee,” Mom coos.

Bea starts to whimper and Mom runs her fingers through Bea’s fine hair.

“Honeybee,” Mom says, “I’m going to need to take off the Band-Aids so I can see the boo-boo.”

Bea whimpers harder. “No,” she says. “It’s gonna hurt too much.”

“Sometimes things need to hurt before they start to feel better,” Mom tells Bea.

The message is for Bea, but I can’t help nodding. That’s exactly it. What I’ve done may cause some hurt, but it’s the only way I have to make things better.

Bea howls when Mom peels off the Band-Aids.

I shut my eyes.

Mom sucks in her breath. “Oh my goodness,” she says. “I can see the marks from his fingers.” I lean over Mom’s shoulder. She’s right—there are bruises shaped like fingers on Bea's skin. "Justine, could you get me my phone?"

First I think Mom wants to call Darlene and tell her what happened. But that isn't why Mom needs her cell. "Turn on all the lights," she tells me after I hand her the phone. "And open the curtains too. We need to get pictures of Bea's shoulder. For evidence."

Mom takes close-up shots, and also some shots from farther away. When Bea fidgets, Mom asks me to hold her so she'll stay still. "These photos are very important," she explains.

"But we need to get ready to go to Dad's house," Bea tells her.

Mom shakes her head. "I can't let you go to your father's house. Not after what's happened . . ."

Bea looks over at me when Mom says that. I nod so Bea will know that everything will be okay. That we've done the right thing.

"Not today," Mom says.

"I don't feel safe at Dad's," I say quietly. It's what Mom wants to hear. As soon as I say it, she smiles. A small smile, and it's gone quickly, but I saw it.

Bea notices too, because she says, "Me neither."

I squeeze Bea's hand again.

Then Bea makes a gulping sound. "What about

Sheldon?" She catches my eyes again. This time, I see panic on her face. I worry that she's going to ruin everything.

Now that the photos are done, Mom pulls Bea onto her lap. "Maybe one day we'll get a cat of our own," Mom says.

"I don't want a cat of our own," Bea says quietly. "I want Sheldon."

Mom rubs her forehead. "Girls," she says, "I need time to think. There's granola on the counter. And almond milk. Why don't you two go have breakfast in the den?"

"In the den?" Bea's face brightens. "What if we make crumbles on the couch?"

"We're not going to worry about crumbles today, Bea. We all need a day off to recover and heal up. Your poor shoulder," Mom says, softly kissing Bea's shoulder before she sets her back down on the floor. "We'll let the boo-boo get some air. Then I'll put on fresh Band-Aids."

I pour the almond milk over our granola and take our bowls to the den. Bea follows at my heels in a way that reminds me of how Sheldon follows her around at Dad's.

I hear Mom whispering on her cell. When she said she needed time to think, it meant she needed to talk to Darlene. I hear snippets of Mom's end of the conversation. "You'll never believe what happened . . . I'm horrified . . . You can see his finger marks . . . I took photographs . . ."

Mom stops talking, but I can hear her tapping on her phone. She must be texting Dad, telling him he won't be getting us this morning. I don't mind spending a quiet day at the condo, but I'll miss seeing Mariella.

"All right," I hear Mom say to Darlene. "Let me read you what I wrote. I took your advice and kept it neutral." Mom drops her voice, but I can still make out what she is saying. "'Alain, I'm keeping the girls with me today. I'm concerned about Bea's shoulder. And Bea will be happier if Justine's around to keep her company.' I didn't get upset, or point out that he can't control his temper. I'll leave that to Maître Pépin."

CHAPTER SEVENTEEN

I can tell from Mom's eyes, which look a little glassy, that she still has a migraine. I can also tell she's trying to ignore it. She's gone from doing nothing to doing everything. I hear clanging in the kitchen. When I go to bring our bowls to the sink, she's kneeling in front of the oven, emptying out the metal drawer underneath. There are pots everywhere, and she's holding a damp cloth like it's a weapon.

Doing stuff around the house calms her down.

A cleaning service comes every second Friday, but they only clean the outsides of things.

"D'you need some help?" I offer.

"No, thanks, sweetheart. You're already a big help with the way you look after Bea. I don't tell you enough how much I appreciate everything you do for your sister. And for me too."

Mom has a point. She doesn't usually thank me for helping with Bea, even though I do more for my little sister than most big sisters do. It's not because Mom isn't grateful—of course she is; it's more because she has so much other stuff to think about.

Mom reaches to the very back of the oven drawer with her cloth.

There's a sheet of paper at Mom's spot at the table. I see Maître Pépin's name at the top, underlined twice. Underneath is a list of points. I scan the list.

1. PHYSICAL ATTACK ON BEA. (PHOTOGRAPHS)
2. TOXIC MOLD IN THE HOUSE.
3. FAILURE TO DO BEA'S READING HOMEWORK.
4.
5.

Numbers four and five are blank. Mom is still working on it.

She stands up to get a dish towel for drying the inside of the drawer. She catches me eyeing her list. She could tell me not to read it, that it's private. But she doesn't. "It must have been awful for you too, sweetheart. To see your sister being hurt like that . . ." she says softly.

I suck in my breath. Should I tell Mom the truth—that Dad had a reason, a good one? What I say now is going to matter a lot . . . and it will affect Mom's case.

Our case.

"It was bad," I say quietly. I close my eyes. I want Mom to think I'm replaying the scene in my head. What I am really doing is trying to imagine a scene I didn't see, a scene that didn't exactly happen. A scene that *could have* happened—and that will help our case. I can see myself tugging on Dad's arm. "I tried to stop him. But he didn't listen."

The dish towel falls out of Mom's hand, and she doesn't bother picking it up. She shakes her head. "I'm sure you tried your best. You always do. But the important thing is that you're safe now. Both of you." She sounds relieved. As if she's pulled us from a burning wreck or swept us out of a tornado's path.

"I love you, Mom."

"I know, sweetheart. I love you too." I can practically feel my heart swelling when she says that.

I go back to the den and find Bea sprawled on the floor with crayons and paper. When she hears me come in, she turns around and holds up a sheet of paper for me to see.

"Come see my picture," she says, waving it in the air like a small flag. "You'll love it!"

"Is that you?" I ask, pointing to what could be a small girl with stick arms and stick legs. She seems to be wearing shorts and a purple T-shirt. Bea hasn't drawn the girl's face. Just the back of her. But I recognize Bea's pigtails.

"Of course it's me," Bea says. "Do you like it?"

At first, I don't understand what the black blob next to Bea is. It's something big, much bigger than her. Are those two stocky legs sticking out from underneath the blob? Is that a small head, and a very long arm? Yes, because now I see there are fingers at the end of the arm, like prongs on a fork. The fingers are reaching for Bea.

"Wow," I say quietly. "You made a drawing of what happened. It's a very good drawing, Bea. You're a real artist."

The compliment makes her beam.

The way Bea keeps watching my face makes me think there is something else in the drawing I'm supposed to notice. But all I see is the figure that is meant to be her, and the blob that is Dad.

"I didn't put Sheldon in," Bea says. "Because Sheldon wasn't even there."

"That's right," I tell Bea. "Sheldon had nothing to do with what happened."

I know it's a good sign that Bea is starting to believe the story we came up with. I pat her head and stroke her hair, and she leans in closer to me.

I'm glad Mom realizes what a good big sister I am.

Bea and Mom both need me.

That makes me feel good.

Even if it's hard sometimes.

"You should sign it," I tell Bea. I point to a white space at the bottom right corner of the paper. "That's where artists usually sign their drawings," I explain.

Bea sorts through her crayons on the floor. "I need a yellow crayon." She makes it sound like it's urgent.

"You can sign in any color," I tell her.

Bea shakes her head. "I need yellow."

I can tell there's no talking her out of it. Besides, there's an old box of crayons at the back of my closet. "I think I know where one is," I tell her. "Give me a minute."

The crayon box is where I thought it was. I don't know why I brought these crayons with me from our old house. I'm too old for crayons. I should give the whole box to Bea. It's when I'm reaching for it that I spot the scrapbook. The one I made in grade three.

I take it out too. On the cover are the words *MY FAMILY.* I read the title out loud. "MY FAMILY."

The scrapbook smells like old glue and some of the pages are stuck together. The top corner of an inside page tears a little when I open it. The first picture is from Mom and Dad's wedding. They both look so young. Dad had a lot more hair. He is lifting the veil from Mom's face and she is laughing so hard her eyes are scrunched up.

Underneath, I've made a heart and written their names. I must've interviewed them, because I included quotes. *Alain: "Your mom really is my better half." Lisa: "There's no one more fun on Planet Earth than your dad."*

On the next page is a Christmas picture. We're all there—even Bea, though she's just a baby bump. Mom's hands are over her belly, so in a way it looks like she is already cradling Bea. We're gathered around a Christmas tree. Dad is wearing the ugly Christmas sweater he wears every year. It's got a reindeer's face on it, and the reindeer's nose is a bright-red pom-pom. Mariella is in the picture too; she's unwrapping a present. And there's Will! I don't see Darlene. She must have been the one taking the photo.

"Justine!" It's Bea coming to check on me. "Did you find a yellow cr— What are you looking at?"

"Just an old scrapbook," I tell her. "From before."

"Before what?"

"Before Mom and Dad stopped getting along."

"They used to get along?" Bea sounds surprised. "Can I see?"

"This picture is from when you were just a baby bump. But you were already cute."

Bea comes to sit next to me. "That's me?" she says, pointing to Mom's tummy.

"That's you."

"Is that from when they sang me that song?" Bea asks.

"Yup."

"Mariella was invited too," Bea says. "Does that mean Mom didn't always hate her?"

"Mom doesn't hate her. It's complicated."

Bea nods as if that makes perfect sense.

When you're in grade three, scrapbooks aren't very big. This one only has three pages. On the last page, there's a picture of just me. Underneath I've written my biography the way you see it on real books. "Read it to me," Bea says when she sees me looking at the page. So I do.

"'Justine Tepper-Lamer lives in the Eastern Townships with her mom and dad. She has a big sister named Mariella, and soon Justine is going to be a big sister too. This is Justine's first book. But she plans to write many more.'"

"What does the red say?" Bea asks. She's pointing to the comment the teacher—I remember her name was

Ms. Odette—made. So I read the comment to Bea too. "'I feel honored to have met your family in this scrapbook, Justine. And I look forward to those other books you are planning to write!'"

"Wow!" Bea says.

"It's just a scrapbook," I tell her as I put it back in its place at the back of the closet.

Bea's face turns serious. "You're not gonna show Mom, are you?"

"I don't think that would be a good idea. You know how she feels about looking backward."

"We're not going that way," Bea and I say at the same time.

I show Bea the box of crayons. "Look what I found. See, the yellow's practically brand-new."

Bea takes the crayon. She has brought her drawing with her. She plops down on the floor and starts on the signature. She's been learning to write her letters. I watch as she struggles to form the letter *B*. "Need some help?" I offer.

"No. I can do it."

I realize Bea isn't trying to make the letter *B*. She has drawn an oval with stripes on it.

"Do you need a black crayon?"

Bea's forehead is wrinkled from concentrating so hard. She is trying to draw a honeybee.

CHAPTER EIGHTEEN

It feels like I'm riding the Goliath.

That's the biggest, scariest roller-coaster at La Ronde. Back in July, Dad took the three of us there. The Goliath was Mariella's idea. Bea was too little for the ride. I offered to stay with her, and let Dad and Mariella go. But Dad said no, that he never really enjoyed roller-coasters. I didn't want Mariella to think I was chicken, so I didn't say that not enjoying roller-coasters might be something else I inherited from him—besides frizzy hair.

The person at the entrance makes you empty your pockets and if you have a purse, you have to leave it behind before you get on. There are wooden crates for people's stuff. Mariella tossed her purse in. I wasn't so sure about leaving my fanny pack because it had my health card and also the ten dollars I'd brought along for souvenir shopping.

"Just leave it," Mariella said. She can be bossy sometimes.

"It's got money in it," I whispered, because I didn't want a thief to get any ideas.

"It's okay, Justine. Leave it."

So I threw my fanny pack into one of the crates. I'm glad I did because it would definitely have fallen off during the ride, and I doubt I'd ever have seen it again.

The Goliath started out slow. Our car chugged uphill, but then it went zooming down, and I had to close my eyes when we went upside down. I squeezed Mariella's hand so hard she had to shake it out afterwards. I didn't know whether to laugh or scream. So I did both.

Mariella had ridden the Goliath before. She'd been to La Ronde with her friends in June. She knew what to expect.

Not me.

When our car got back to the docking station, my head was spinning. Mariella had to help me get out. Her purse and my fanny pack were right where we'd left them. My ten dollars was safe inside.

Mariella's eyes were glowing. "Let's go again!"

I said I didn't want to. I didn't admit that I'd worried our car was going to fly off the rails. I told Mariella I didn't want Dad and Bea to have to keep waiting around.

Here's why it feels like I'm back on the Goliath: Things

around me are starting to move so quickly I can't keep track of them. Also, I don't know whether to laugh hysterically or scream.

First thing Monday morning, Mom phoned Maître Pépin. He already knew about the mold. But he was *very concerned* (those were Mom's words when I heard her talking to Darlene afterward) about the *violent episode.* Most of all, he was concerned when he heard that Bea and I don't feel safe around Dad. Even if it meant my plan was working, I started to feel guilty. Maybe I went too far.

After that, things started moving even faster—like when the roller-coaster reached the top and we were about to go down the hill really fast. And I worried the car might fly off the rails. This is the thing: You can't get off the Goliath once you're on it.

After school on Monday, Mom had news for us. She had put out a plate of sliced cheese and grapes for us all to snack on—and I was glad to see her nibbling too. "Maître Pépin thinks you two should have your own lawyer."

"Our own lawyer? Why can't he be our lawyer?" I asked Mom.

Mom popped a red grape into her mouth. She chewed and swallowed it before speaking. "Because that isn't how these things work. It's Maître Pépin's recommendation.

So I went ahead and set up an appointment with a lawyer who specializes in representing children. You're going to meet with him on Friday morning. I know it's a lot for you girls to have to deal with. But it's all for the best. Thank goodness there's a system in place to help us." I had the feeling Mom wasn't just glad about the system. She was also glad our case was moving forward. All because of me. That thought made me feel proud—and it made the guilty feelings less sharp.

"Lots of children are in danger when they're with one of their parents," Mom added. "That's why there are special lawyers for kids."

In danger with one of their parents?

That's when the guilt got sharp again. Even sharper than before. I'm the one who made Mom think that. Dad's negligent sometimes, but he's not dangerous.

But how can I tell my mom that getting on the Goliath might have been a mistake?

ooo

On Wednesday night, I hear Mom tell Darlene that Dad likes the idea of our having our own lawyer—that it will help get to the *bottom of things*.

Whatever that means. Mom definitely seems psyched

about the latest developments. And I'm glad for that. Besides, it's too late to get off the roller-coaster.

Bea is excited about not having to go to pre-K on Friday morning. Our appointment with the lawyer isn't until 10 a.m., but Mom says there's no point in us going to school for just an hour and a half.

That day, Bea comes to my room and wakes me up early. So much for sleeping in!

I groan when she buzzes in my ear. "Go away, Bea."

Bea doesn't listen. Instead, she crawls into my bed. I pull her close. "I don't have pre-K," Bea says.

"I know. And I don't have school. That's why we're supposed to be sleeping in."

When we wake up for the second time, the sun is streaming through the slats in my window blinds, making zebra stripes on my comforter.

"Bea?" I hear Mom shout. Even though Mom's only said one syllable, I can tell she's anxious. Why am I so tuned in to her feelings? Is it the same for all daughters? "Bea? Where are you?" Mom must've gone into Bea's room to wake her up.

"She's with me," I call out. "Everything's okay."

Mom is already at my doorway. She's dressed the same as she was for our family photo. She's blow-dried her hair and put on makeup. Maybe Mom's meeting our lawyer too.

Mom's face softens when she looks at us, snuggled together. She claps. "All right, then, let's get this show on the road, girls!"

Because Mom's wearing her checked blouse and black skirt, I ask if she wants us to wear what we wore for our family photo. Mom rubs the tip of her nose the way she does when she's about to make an important decision. "No, I don't think so. I wouldn't want your lawyer to think I'm forcing you two to be matchy."

Bea sits up on her elbows. "You forced us to be matchy for the photo."

Mom laughs. "It's true," she tells Bea. "But that was different."

Bea gets out of my bed and starts bopping. "Can I wear lip gloss?"

"No way!" Mom says.

While Bea brushes her teeth, I ask Mom whether Bea and I will be together for our meeting with the lawyer.

"I didn't think of that," Mom says. Which surprises me since she usually thinks of everything. "But if you want to be together, sweetheart, we'll ask the lawyer to do it that way."

"Phew." I didn't mean to say it out loud.

Mom gives me a sideways look. So I'm relieved when all she says is, "Come to think of it, I like the idea of Bea having you there."

CHAPTER NINETEEN

Our lawyer isn't what I expected.

For one thing, he has an earring in his left ear. He's wearing red Converse high-tops, and there's a dragon tattoo on his forearm. He tells us we can call him Fred. "Not Maître?" I ask. "Or Maître Fred? Are you sure?"

"Just Fred is fine." He winks at me when he says that. Are lawyers allowed to wink?

Bea can't take her eyes off Fred's tattoo. "My mom says tattoos are gross. That when people who get tattoos grow up, they'll be sorry they got one." She shakes her head the way Mom does. Which makes me feel bad for her. I want Bea to stay Bea for always, and not turn into somebody else.

Bea might look like Mom, but she definitely has her own personality. I hope that even when she grows up, Bea will stay warm and light—if you can say that about a person—and always a little bit silly.

"I'm grown-up," Fred tells her. "And I'm not sorry I got one."

Bea reaches out to touch Fred's arm. "Is it a dragon?"

"Yup," Fred says. *Yup?* I hope Fred won't speak like that to the judge.

"Some dragons breathe fire," Bea says.

Fred laughs. "Not this one. This one's a friendly dragon."

"Phew," Bea says.

Fred isn't sitting behind his desk. He's in an armchair, with Bea and me across from him on a small gray sofa with orange pillows. The faded upholstery makes me think that a lot of other kids must have sat here before us. I wonder if they all needed their own lawyer because they were in danger from one of their parents.

"It's good to meet the two of you." Fred says it like he means it.

"Do you want to see my shoulder?" Bea asks. She gets up from the sofa and pulls at the edge of her T-shirt. "Dad did it."

"Bea," I whisper, "we're supposed to wait for Fred to ask us questions."

I can feel Fred watching us. There's a turquoise file folder and a pen on his lap. But he hasn't opened the folder or taken the cap off the pen.

"Thanks for your help, Justine," Fred says to me. That makes me feel very grown-up. "I do want to see your shoulder, Bea, but maybe we could get to know each other a little first. You good with that?"

Bea plops back down on the love seat. "Sure. I'm four. How old are you?"

"Bea!" I say.

Bea shrugs. "What did I do now?"

"You're not supposed to ask grown-ups their age. It's not polite." To be honest, I'd also like to know Fred's age. I'm not sure he's old enough to be a real lawyer.

"I'm thirty-one." Fred opens the turquoise folder and pops the cap off his pen. "So Bea, you're four. And Justine, you're twelve, correct?"

"Correct."

Fred jots that down on the sheet of paper inside the file folder. I feel better now that he's taking notes.

"So first of all, I need you girls to understand that as your lawyer, my job is to help you tell the court what *you* want. Before we get to that, I thought we could talk a little about your parents' divorce and how it's been impacting you."

"Imp . . . ?" It's another new word for Bea.

"How Mom and Dad's divorce makes us feel," I tell her.

"I wish they could get married again," Bea says. "Then everything would be fine."

I'm surprised when Bea says that. She was so little when Mom and Dad split up I didn't think she could remember what it was like when we all lived together. But Fred nods as if what Bea just said makes perfect sense. "What things aren't fine?" he asks Bea. He rests his pen on the crease in the file folder.

"It isn't fine that we have two houses. Well, one's a condo," Bea says.

"Can I say what isn't fine?" I ask Fred.

"Of course you can, Justine. What isn't fine?"

I give him a moment to pick up his pen again because what I'm about to tell him is extremely important. When Fred doesn't pick up his pen, I say it anyway.

"It isn't fine that Dad's house is moldy. It isn't fine that we have to share one bathroom. Especially not for a girl my age." I pause, because I know I have to add this next part. "And it isn't fine that he hurt Bea. For no reason."

Fred nods, but he doesn't say anything.

"Shouldn't you write that down?" I ask him.

"I generally like to chat a bit with my clients before I take notes," Fred says. "I can see you're very organized, Justine."

"Thank you. I am."

"She is," Bea says at the same time. "Like Mom."

"I can also see you two are very close," Fred says. "I'm glad you have each other."

"We also have a big sister. Though she isn't one hundred percent," Bea says.

Fred looks confused, so I explain. "Bea means Mariella. She's our half sister. She's from our dad's first marriage. We're very close with her too. Especially me."

Bea pokes me with her elbow. "Me too!"

"I was wondering," Fred says, looking only at me this time, "do you have anything good to tell me about your dad?"

Fred's question catches me by surprise—like when some kid at recess throws a ball, only you didn't notice, so you jump when it lands in front of you.

I'm trying to come up with the right answer. Maybe I focus so much on the things Dad does wrong that I don't think about what he does right. Then again, what *does* he do right?

"He doesn't remind me to put on my seat belt." The words just pop out—even though they don't answer Fred's question.

"He doesn't have to," Bea points out. "He has *you* to remind him."

When Fred chuckles, it reminds me of something good about Dad. "Dad's funny," I say. "Though it's embarrassing when he laughs at his own jokes."

Bea raises her hand. "I know something else good about Dad."

Fred picks up his pen again. "What's that?"

"He loves us," Bea says.

Fred turns back to me. "Would you agree with that?"

I can't say no. *Of course* Dad loves us. He has to. We're his daughters. Just like we have to love him because he's our dad. But right now, more than anything else, I need to help Mom. Not just because I want her to win her case. Our case. But also because I know if she gets what she wants, she'll stop being anxious, and I won't have to worry about her falling apart again.

I know I can't just go ahead and say I don't think Dad loves us. So instead I say, "Yes . . . but . . ."

Fred waits for me to say more. He looks at me, then clicks his pen. "But what?"

"Dad loves us, but he doesn't always do such a good job taking care of us."

It's a good answer—especially considering I had to come up with it on the spot—and I'm glad when Bea nods. I hope Fred noticed.

"What do you mean when you say your dad doesn't always do such a good job taking care of you?" Fred wants to know. There's something soft in his eyes I didn't see before. That's when I realize he really wants to help us. This meeting is going super well.

"All the stuff I told you before. The mold, the one bathroom . . ." The next part is the hardest to say, but I know I have to. "And especially the violent episode."

"'Violent episode,'" Fred repeats.

"Can I show you my shoulder now?" Bea asks.

"Okay, I'm ready," Fred tells her.

Bea bounces up from the sofa again. This time, when she pulls down the top edge of her T-shirt, Fred takes a look. "That's a lot of Band-Aids," he says.

"Mom's been changing them," Bea explains. "She says boo-boos need air."

"We took pictures," I add.

Why does Fred look surprised? Shouldn't a lawyer understand how important it is to have evidence? "*We?*" he asks.

"Yeah," I tell him. "We. Mom took the pictures. But I held Bea. Mom couldn't hold Bea and take pictures at the same time."

"Of course." Fred writes something down on his sheet.

"There's more evidence," I say. I'm feeling more grown-up by the second.

"There is?" Again, Fred sounds surprised.

"I brought one of Bea's drawings." I reach for my backpack, which is on the floor next to my side of the sofa.

I take out the drawing.

Bea looks on proudly. "I made it," she tells Fred.

"After the violent episode," I add.

Fred studies the drawing without saying a word.

"That's Dad grabbing me for no reason," Bea says.

Fred lays his file folder on the floor. Then he puts his hands on his knees and leans in so that he's a few inches closer to Bea. "I'm sorry that happened to you, Bea." Then he turns to me. "Did you see the whole thing?"

I can't let Fred see I'm nervous. I want to take a deep breath, but I don't. "Yes," I tell him. Then, though I didn't feel it coming, I start to get choked up.

There's a Kleenex box on the table next to where Fred is sitting. He reaches over and pushes the box toward me. "It must have been hard for you too, Justine."

I grab a Kleenex and blow my nose into it. "It is," I say. "I mean, it was. Very hard."

"Is there something you want me to do with this drawing?" Fred asks me.

I take a deep breath. "Could you show it to the judge?"

"Sure," Fred says. "I could do that for you."

"That means it's a good drawing, right?" Bea asks.

"It's very good," Fred answers.

"There's other evidence too," I tell Fred.

"There is?" Bea asks.

My notebook is tucked away in its usual place at the bottom of my backpack. This will be the first time I've shown it to anyone. The time Solange and Jeannine saw it doesn't count because I didn't want them reading it.

"I've been keeping notes," I explain as I take the notebook out.

CHAPTER TWENTY

Fred says what a nice notebook it is. He likes the pale-pink cover and the way I personalized it by adding the silver stick-on stars. He opens it to the first page. I watch his eyes travel from left to right, then back to the left. Why is he chewing on his lip? When he gets to the end of the first entry, he looks up at me. "You take good notes, Justine. I imagine that's pretty unusual for someone your age."

"Thank you." I nearly tell him how much I love writing. But I don't want to waste time. Mom explained how she and Dad are splitting Fred's bill. Lawyers charge a fortune. They even charge for phone calls! It's a good thing Darlene doesn't charge for those, or we'd be broke!

Fred watches my face. He's trying to figure out something about me. Why doesn't he just go ahead and ask?

Then he does.

"Did someone give you this notebook, Justine?"

It's an easy question. "My mom bought it for me," I tell him. "Downtown."

"I never saw that book before," Bea says. "Why didn't Mom get *me* one? A purple one."

There's a two-story bookstore on the busiest section of Sainte-Catherine Street downtown. It's between our two big department stores: Simons and La Baie. It was just me and Mom that day, which hardly ever happens. Bea was at a birthday party. So for a treat, Mom took me downtown.

We had high tea at the Birks building. When Mom was growing up, Birks was the fanciest jewelry store in Montreal. Over the years, it's gotten smaller, so now there's a tearoom in the extra space.

A waiter wearing a tuxedo and white gloves served us mini-sandwiches with the crusts cut off, and petits fours for dessert. Petits fours are tiny pastries. Ours had pink and blue icing. We had tea from a silver teapot. I didn't say but the tea tasted the same as the kind you make from a grocery store teabag.

Afterward, we walked over to the bookstore. We both love reading, and the bookstore is a five-minute walk from the Birks building.

They sell a lot of stuff besides books. That bothers Mom.

"Pillows at a bookstore! What's this world coming to?" she said.

Some of the pillows were shaggy and a beautiful golden-beige color. I hope they still sell them when I'm a grown-up with my own condo one day.

Besides the pillows, blankets and picture frames, there were aisles of greeting cards. Those didn't bug Mom the way the pillows did, though she considers store-bought greeting cards a waste of money. Mom has strong opinions—even about pillows and greeting cards. Usually I feel the same way. Almost like it's automatic. Maybe that happens to all kids whose parents have strong opinions. Or do some of those kids ever object and say, "No way, I disagree! Pillows in a bookstore rule!"

Mom didn't have any complaints about the journals aisle. Probably because she knows how much writing matters to me, and she's proud of my English marks. It's always been my best subject, probably because I like words so much.

"Why don't you go ahead and pick one?" Mom said.

"For real?" She doesn't believe in buying us *extras*. She's always saying how most North American kids have too much stuff.

"For real. Writers need to write. And you've always been a writer, Justine."

That made me feel super proud.

Choosing wasn't easy. I didn't just pick this one for the color. I also liked that it had a silky pink ribbon that marks the page I'm on.

Mom didn't even check the price. "I want you to have a book you'll feel like writing in. Aren't you and Bea going to your dad's next weekend?" Mom asked me.

The question took me by surprise. Mom knows our visitation schedule the way I know exactly what time the bells ring at my school.

There's always a line-up to pay at the bookstore. And there are bins with what Dad once told me are called *novelty items*. Things you never planned to buy, but when you see them, you suddenly want them. Dad says it's smart marketing to have novelty items by the checkout.

Mom saw me eyeing a packet of silver stick-on stars in one of the bins. "It's a novelty item," I told her. I didn't say who taught me that expression.

But I think she knew. "It's also called an impulse buy," she said. "Impulsive people buy things they don't need." So I could hardly believe when she said I could have the stars too.

It wasn't until we were taking the revolving doors back out to Sainte-Catherine Street that Mom said, "You can use your journal to take notes." She lifted her voice for the words *take notes*.

I'm in the middle of remembering that afternoon with Mom when Fred's voice brings me back to his office, his tattooed forearm and the small gray sofa with Bea next to me. "I have to ask you something important, Justine," Fred is saying.

"Sure. What?"

Fred is watching my face again. "Was it your own idea to take all these notes?"

I swallow. "Yup."

It's not a lie. At least I don't think it is.

CHAPTER TWENTY-ONE

Fred leans toward us and rests his hands on his knees. "So, Justine and Bea, I think now's a good time for you girls to tell me what *you* want. So I can tell the judge on your behalf."

I take a deep breath. Even if my mom is opinionated, even if she's sometimes hard on me, I'm the only one who can help her. If I don't, she might fall apart all over again. I need to do this now. "We want our father to have reduced access."

Bea nods, even though I can guarantee she has no idea what *reduced access* even means.

"So, to be clear, you're saying you want to spend *less* time with your dad than you already do?"

"Yes," I answer again for both of us. "We don't feel safe with him."

Fred turns to Bea. "Is that how you feel too, Bea? That you're not safe with your dad?"

"Yes," Bea says. Her voice sounds smaller than usual, as if it's coming from a room down the hall.

Even if our appointment still seems to be going super well, there's one thing worrying me. That Fred will want to speak to Bea alone. When I'm in the room with her, I know Bea will agree with whatever I say. But I don't know what'll happen if I'm not there.

I'm trying *not* to ask Fred if he needs to talk to just Bea. If I ask, I might give him the idea. Better just to see how things go.

Fred jots down more notes. When he looks up and catches me eyeing his clock, he says, "We're nearly done."

"So you don't need to talk to us separately?"

Fred gives me that wondering look he gave me before. "Do you think I *should* talk to you separately?"

It's a trick question. If I say no, it might make Fred want to do it. "Whatever you think is best."

Fred turns back to Bea. "I know you're a very smart kid, Bea. Probably the smartest four-year-old I ever met."

Bea crosses her hands on her lap. "Really? Thank you."

"However, Bea, you won't be coming to court." Fred has slowed down, now that he's getting to the legal stuff. "Even though you're super smart, four-year-olds don't get to testify."

Bea looks at me. She doesn't know what *testify* means. "It means talk to the judge," I explain.

"That's right," Fred says. "Four-year-olds don't get to talk to the judge. But twelve-year-olds sometimes do. Justine, are you up for that?"

"I am," I say.

"Justine is even smarter than me," Bea adds.

"All right, then," Fred says as he closes his file folder and puts the cap back on his pen. "Is there anything else either of you want to ask me—or tell me—before we wrap up?"

"No," I answer, tugging on Bea's hand as we get up from the sofa. If we don't get out of here soon, Bea could say something that might ruin our case.

Bea shakes my hand loose. She raises her index finger in the air to signal she's got something else to say. I suck in my breath. This could be bad.

"It was nice meeting you," she tells Fred.

I am so relieved I laugh. When I finish laughing, I come up with a question for Fred. Why didn't I think of it before?

"Can I have my journal back? Or do you need it for the judge?"

"Thanks for reminding me, Justine. Of course you can have it back. But if it's okay with you, I'd like to photocopy a few pages. Do I have your permission to do that?"

"Of course." I feel honored. Fred understands my notes are important.

There's a photocopier outside his office. I thank Fred when he returns my notebook. I let go of Bea's hand so I can jam the notebook back at the bottom of my backpack. "I can bring it to court," I tell Fred. "Maybe the judge will want to read the whole thing."

Fred nods. He's watching my face again. "Maybe," he says.

Mom dropped us off before the appointment while she went to find parking. She's in the waiting area now, chatting with the receptionist. I wonder if they could become friends. You never know, and Mom could use more friends. She pretty much just has Darlene, and that's basically a phone friendship now. Maybe the receptionist lives near us.

"Mom!" Bea calls out. You'd think they'd been separated for months.

Mom squats down and opens her arms for a hug. Then she gets up to shake Fred's hand. She calls him Maître Loisel. "His name is just Fred," Bea whispers. "He has a tattoo and he doesn't regret it."

Mom doesn't ask Fred how the appointment went, or mention the bill. It must be hard for her to keep those questions in.

"I've heard you're a wonderful advocate for children,"

she tells Fred. "It must be satisfying to do that sort of work. Thank you so much for helping m—" Mom stops herself. "Justine and Bea."

Mom flashes Fred a movie star smile. She saves those for important people. Fred smiles back. "You're right about my work. It's very satisfying. And you've got special girls," he says. "I'm glad to have the opportunity to represent them."

Mom shifts her weight from one foot to the other. It's not something she usually does, though Dad does it all the time. "If you don't mind my asking," she says to Fred, "what happens next?"

"Maître Pépin will advise you once we have a court date," Fred tells her.

Mom shakes Fred's hand again and flashes him another smile. "Thank you again, Maître Loisel . . . um, Fred."

On the drive back to school, Mom still doesn't ask how the appointment went. She must be dying to know. She likes knowing everything—especially if it has to do with us, and even more so if it has to do with us and Dad.

"We told Fred we want to spend less time with Dad." I say it like it's no big deal.

"Thank you," Mom says. Is she thanking me for filling her in, or because she's grateful for what we told Fred? Maybe both.

The car in front of us is veering out of its lane. Mom honks.

There's a flash of red lights when the driver hits his brakes. Mom hits her brakes too. I look behind us. Luckily, there's no car close by.

But Bea flies forward. There's a small clunk as her head makes contact with the back of the passenger seat.

Mom keeps her eyes on the road. "Oh my God, honeybee," she says, without turning around. "Are you all right?" Then, in a higher voice, she asks, "Justine, is she all right?"

Bea doesn't say anything. But I'm pretty sure she's fine. She just looks a little stunned. "Does your head hurt?" I ask her.

"It went bump," she says. "But it didn't hurt. Not really."

"Phew," I say. "It's good you have a hard head."

I expect Mom to be relieved too. But she isn't. She's angry. And not at the driver whose fault it was. At me.

"Why didn't you check the buckle on your sister's car seat?" Mom's voice is so loud that even with the car windows closed, if there was anyone outside, they'd hear her.

"I thought I did," I say.

"Thinking you did isn't good enough. Your sister obviously wasn't properly buckled in."

There's no point arguing with Mom when she gets like this. So I swallow the words I am thinking before they can leave my mouth.

Why is it always my fault?

I'm only twelve.

I love Bea more than anything. But I'm her sister.

Not her mother.

Aren't mothers supposed to be the ones to check that their children are properly buckled in?

CHAPTER TWENTY-TWO

Saturday, Oct. 20

Dear Pink Notebook,

You must be wondering why I turned you upside down and started writing on your very last page.

Here's the answer: It just felt right. Like I had to. Maybe because I'm feeling upside down myself.

I don't want to start keeping a list of the things Mom does wrong.

I'm not even sure I want to keep writing a list of the things Dad does wrong.

Maybe the problem is I spend too much time thinking about my parents.

So here's a list of how I'm feeling.

Angry.

Angry because Mom keeps blaming me for stuff that isn't my fault.

Also angry because I feel like I have to hold my anger in.

Which makes me even angrier.

Writing this helped. A little, anyhow.

But I have to put you away now, Pink Notebook. I'm leaving for Jeannine's. You're not going to believe this, but Mom said yes to me sleeping over there. And Solange is sleeping over too!

Mom's opposed to sleepovers. Except for emergencies—like the time I slept over at Leonor and Mariella's. Mom worries other parents won't provide adequate supervision or that there'll be only junk food to eat.

But she agreed to let me sleep over at Jeannine's. On the condition that she could speak to Jeannine's mom beforehand.

"Do you really have to?" I asked her.

"Of course I have to. You don't think I'm going to let you sleep over at some strange people's house, do you?"

I groaned. "Jeannine's parents aren't strange people. Her dad's an accountant and her mom's a nurse."

"A nurse?" Mom liked that. Probably in case I came down with a mysterious and possibly life-threatening disease on Saturday night. Luckily, Mom talked to Jeannine's mom and decided Jeannine's parents weren't ax-murderers.

Jeannine, Solange and I are going to stay up and talk all night long. I also look forward to getting to see another family up close. I figure it'll be interesting.

And it is.

Jeannine's parents are the gardener type. I can tell right away.

They don't come to the door when Solange and I show up. Only Jeannine does. Her parents are stretched out on the L-shaped couch in the living room, reading the Saturday paper. I notice their toes touching.

Jeannine doesn't make us take off our shoes when we come in. Her parents must not mind a little grit on the floor. When Jeannine introduces us, her parents don't get up from the couch. They just lower their sections of the paper and call out that it's nice to meet us, and that Solange and I should make ourselves at home.

"Are there any house rules we should know about?" I ask them.

When they laugh at my question, I know for sure they're gardeners.

They tell us we can order any kind of pizza we want for lunch (the crust doesn't have to be whole wheat), and they let us drink Coke. I don't admit to my friends that it's my first sip of Coke *ever* because I'm afraid they'll laugh at me. But when I taste it, I decide I haven't missed much. It's so sweet it hurts my teeth.

I figure we'll spend the afternoon hanging out, but then Jeannine asks her parents if they can drive us to the Fairview shopping mall, and her mom says, "Sure, why not? We're in the mood for a drive." I wonder if they'll stay with us—or just drop us off. I hear Mom's voice in my head: *Twelve year-olds should not be left unsupervised at a shopping mall.*

Shh, I tell the voice. *Quit telling me what to do all the time.*

I don't ask if Jeannine's parents will be supervising. Besides, part of me is dying to know how it would feel to hang out at the mall with my two best friends—without grown-ups watching our every move.

Which is why I'm disappointed when Jeannine's dad looks for a space in the parking lot. So much for that taste of freedom I was imagining!

It turns out Jeannine's parents aren't planning to do much supervising. More like *supervising-lite.*

"I'm dying for a latté," Jeannine's mom announces as she gets out of the van.

"There's a Starbucks in the food court. Let's grab a coffee while the girls do their thing," Jeannine's dad tells her.

Do our thing? Really? Yay!

Mom would nix that plan in a nanosecond. But all Jeannine's mom says is, "I love Saturdays."

We all walk to the food court because Jeannine's parents want us to know where they'll be. I wonder if they'll hold hands—I like when grown-ups hold hands—but they don't. They walk close to each other, though, and neither one goes ahead of the other, the way I remember my parents doing before they got divorced.

Jeannine's parents stake out an empty table. When we leave, they are standing together at the Starbucks counter. Jeannine's mom must have said something funny, because we hear Jeannine's dad's belly laugh from across the food court. "Why does he have to laugh so loudly?" Jeannine says, but you can tell she doesn't really mind. It would be nice to have parents who got along. I can't remember ever hearing Dad laugh at one of Mom's jokes. Not that Mom ever made a lot of jokes. Maybe gardeners are funnier than carpenters.

The mall has more than two hundred stores, but

Jeannine and Solange only care about Sephora. When I look in the window of a bookstore called BookNook, Jeannine rolls her eyes and says, "What's wrong with you, girl? This isn't a school day!"

I laugh when Solange loops her arms through ours and drags us toward Sephora's black-and-silver doors. My friends are right. I'll think about books another time.

It's my first time in a Sephora. I've poked around the makeup section at the drugstore, but this is different. This is a giant place with nothing but makeup and beauty products. It feels like I'm entering another world, a world I'm not quite old enough for . . . but almost.

The store is packed. The customers all have hot-pink plastic shopping baskets, many half-full with tubes and little cardboard boxes. There are mirrors everywhere, and customers perched on tall chrome stools, their heads tilted back or to the side, eyes closed, while a makeup artist does their makeup. The artists—there are dozens—wear red-and-black aprons. Some are so beautiful they could be runway models; others look like they're going out for Halloween, their eyes rimmed in fluorescent blue or purple or yellow. I would never let someone wearing fake eyelashes and bright-yellow eyeshadow do my makeup!

There's a whole aisle of skincare products. The expensive

brands are at the back. Because Jeannine knows her way around, she heads for the house-brand makeup. She says we could never afford the luxury products anyway.

"We should stick together," I tell my friends. I haven't told them I've never been inside a Sephora, so I try to make it sound like I'm looking out for them, when truth is, I don't want to get lost in this world where I don't quite belong.

Sephora is Mariella's favorite store. She says makeup is a form of self-expression. Thinking about Mariella makes something in my chest hurt. This would be even more fun with her! I bet she's friends with some of the makeup artists. Mariella can make friends with anybody.

I haven't seen her for nearly three weeks. We text, but it's not the same. Not the same at all.

That's when the weirdest thing happens.

"Justine!"

It's Mariella's voice.

It's like I called her—and she answered.

There she is, standing at the end of the next aisle, near a chrome stool. One of her friends must be getting her makeup done.

"Mariella!" I call out as I elbow my way through the crowd of shoppers toward her.

Jeannine and Solange follow me. They've heard so much

about my glamorous, sporty half sister they must want to see her as much as I do.

"Is that Mariella getting her makeup done?" Jeannine calls out from behind me. "Maybe she'll let us watch."

"No," I say without turning around. "It must be one of her friends. Mariella has two zillion friends." Saying that makes me feel like I'm the popular one.

It's better that Mariella's not getting her makeup done. If she was, she wouldn't be able to talk, and I really want Solange and Jeannine to meet her. I've missed Mariella a lot, but I didn't realize how much until this second. I couldn't have a better, more fun big sister.

Mariella drops her shopping basket to the floor and rushes toward me. I'm happy she loves me as much as I love her. "Justine!" she says again, wrapping her arms around me.

"*Bon Dieu!* Good God!" a voice says.

It's Mariella's friend—the one getting her makeup done. Mariella has a lot of French-speaking friends.

Except that voice can only belong to one person: Grandmami.

How did I miss the red cape?

Grandmami turns to look at me. "Ma'am," the makeup artist says, "please try not to move."

Grandmami ignores her. "You don't understand. It's Justine. *Ma petite fille*. My granddaughter."

The makeup artist hands her a Kleenex. "Please, ma'am . . . your eye makeup."

Grandmami bounces up from her stool, and for a second I wonder if that's where Bea gets all her bopping from. "I don't give a damn about my *maquillage*! This is the first time I've seen my *petite fille* in nearly three weeks!"

I'm expecting another hug. But Grandmami just looks at me for what feels like ages—and smiles. As if she likes everything she sees. As if she's not just looking at my outside, but my inside too. Then she pulls me in for a long hug.

When the hug finally ends, Grandmami turns to Jeannine and Solange. "You must be Justine's dearest friends," Grandmami says. "In this life, friends are as necessary as water—and *oxygène*."

"You don't look like anybody's grandmother," Solange says.

Grandmami laughs. "Thank goodness for that."

The makeup artist taps Grandmami's shoulder. "Ma'am," she says, "give me five more minutes. I haven't finished with your eyes." It's true that Grandmami's eyelids are chalky white.

"*Je m'en fous*," Grandmami says, which means, "What do

I care?" "I refuse to miss a moment of this delightful girl's company," she says, looking at me the way she did before, "and the company of her two fine friends."

Another customer is waiting to get her makeup done. "Girls," Grandmami says to us, "I want you each to pick out something you'd like from this lovely store."

"Us too?" Solange asks.

"*Mais oui!*" Grandmami says. "I'll meet you all at the cash register."

CHAPTER TWENTY-THREE

"Is your grandmother super rich?" Jeannine wants to know.

"I'm not sure, but I don't think so."

Just as she promised, Grandmami is waiting at the cash. Another woman has stopped to talk to her. "If you don't mind my asking, what eyeshadow is that you're wearing?" the woman says.

"I think Grandmami might be starting a new trend," Mariella whispers to me.

Grandmami doesn't check the price tags on the items we've chosen. She just hands the cashier her credit card. "What about *échantillons*, my dear? Samples, surely you have some," she says to the cashier.

The cashier rummages through a box and hands Grandmami two small bottles that look like they have shampoo inside. "I need two more," she says. "One for each of my girls."

"Thanks, Grandmami," Solange says when Grandmami hands her one of the bottles.

Grandmami laughs. She likes that Solange called her Grandmami.

"We have one last errand," Grandmami announces. "I have a special treat in mind—for Justine."

"You do?" I say. "But you've already spoiled me a lot. And my friends too." Mom thinks spoiling kids makes them feel entitled. But I push that thought away. It helps that Grandmami is distracting me with her comments about the displays in the store windows we are passing.

"Do you think I'm much too old for those jeans?" she asks, pointing to a pair of faded jeans with torn knees.

"Not much too old," Mariella tells her. "Just a little bit too old."

Grandmami thinks that's hilarious. "Look at that," she says, pointing to a fluorescent orange bikini as we pass a swimsuit store. "It's your color, Justine. There aren't many women who can wear such a bold shade."

"My mother would never—" I stop myself. Why is it that even when she isn't with me, I hear Mom's voice in my head? And why is she always trying to spoil my fun?

Solange tugs on my arm. "What do you think the special treat is?"

Grandmami has good hearing for an old woman because though she is walking four feet ahead, she answers Solange's question. "Why don't I give you a clue? The answer goes *ring ring*. And it's not found at a jewelry store!"

"I bet it's a phone!" Jeannine says. "Justine, I think Grandmami wants to buy you a phone." Jeannine sounds as excited as I am. She knows how much I want a phone. She also knows how my mother feels about twelve-year-olds with cellphones because she adds, in a really low whisper that even Grandmami can't hear, "You don't have to tell your mom."

There's a Bell store at Fairview, which is where we end up. "When we're done," Jeannine says to Grandmami, "could you come say *bonjour* to my parents? They'd be thrilled to meet you."

"*Absolument!*" Grandmami says. "I adore meeting new people. My last husband—may his soul rest in peace—used to say I was like a dog. Always wagging my tail and eager to sniff a new bottom!"

"Grandmami!" I say, because this time she has gone too far with her jokes. But Mariella and my friends must not think so because they are cracking up.

"Can you believe what she just said?" Jeannine asks me and Solange. Then she turns to Grandmami. "You should have your own TV show!"

"How many husbands have you had?" Solange asks Grandmami. My ears prick up. I never thought of asking Grandmami that. But she did just say "my last husband." So she must have had more than one.

I worry the question will make Grandmami sad, but it doesn't. She winks at Solange. "Let's just say I've had more than one . . . and fewer than six!"

"Oh my God!" Jeannine squeals.

"See that fellow behind the counter?" Grandmami says as the five of us walk into the Bell store. "That," she goes on, lowering her voice so the cute young guy behind the counter won't hear, "could be my next husband!"

Even I crack up. I've never seen Solange and Jeannine laugh so hard. At the rate things are going, Jeannine might end up inviting Grandmami to our sleepover!

"Good afternoon, sir," Grandmami says to the salesman. "I want to buy my granddaughter a cellphone. And get her a cellphone plan."

"Grandmami," I say, "are you sure? That's expensive. And my mom—"

"Of course I'm sure," Grandmami says. "I always got along well with your mother, *chérie*. She means well. And I happen to agree that twelve is young to have a phone. But I've noticed that for someone your age, you have many,

many responsibilities. Adult responsibilities, in fact. I believe a cellphone could prove useful. Besides, you're nearly thirteen."

I nod when Grandmami says that. I do have many responsibilities. I'm glad Grandmami noticed.

She gets a mischievous look in her eyes. "Anyhow," she says, "next time that father of yours stops talking to me, I'll have someone to call!"

Which is how I end up with a cellphone and a monthly plan that Grandmami is going to pay for. She even lets me pick my own case. There are a lot to choose from. There's a pale-pink one that would match with my notebook.

But in the end, I choose one that's covered with pictures of pens and pencils.

"I'd have picked the one with unicorns," Solange says.

Grandmami understands why I chose the pens and pencils. "Justine loves to write," she tells the cute salesman.

Jeannine's parents fall for Grandmami too. They are planning a trip to France and they have loads of questions they want to ask her.

Mariella offers to show me how to add her phone number to my contacts list. She also shows me how to mute the phone so my mom won't hear it ring. Then she looks up at me. "Are you and Bea doing okay?" she asks.

"We're fine," I say, but I don't look her in the eye.

"It must be hard not seeing us. It's hard for me."

"Not seeing you is the hardest," I tell her. I can feel a lump in my throat, but I don't want to cry. I hold up my phone. "At least now I'll be able to text you whenever I want. What about Dad? How's he doing?"

"Not so good," she says. "He says he misses you and Bea so much it hurts. He says it feels like a part of him's been amputated."

I wince. "Amputated? Poor Dad," I say. And I mean it. "What about Sheldon? How's he?"

Mariella sucks in her breath.

For a second, I worry that something's wrong with the cat. If there is, what will I tell Bea?

But there's nothing wrong with Sheldon.

"Remember that cold I had—the one that wouldn't go away?" Mariella asks me. "Two weekends ago I was at Dad's, and I coughed so hard I had trouble breathing. My mother took me to the doctor, who sent me for allergy tests . . . It turns out I have a severe allergy to cats. We're going to have to find another home for Sheldon."

"You are?!" My voice breaks. If Sheldon goes to live with another family, will Bea ever get to see him again? "Do you think you'll find someone to take him?"

Mariella makes a sound that is somewhere between a laugh and a sob. She loves Sheldon too. “There aren’t too many people,” she says, “who want a one-eyed cat.”

CHAPTER TWENTY-FOUR

Jeannine's mom knocks on the bedroom door. "It's lights out now, girls!" she announces.

All three of us are in Jeannine's double bed. We've been talking about everything—school; our favorite books, movies and music; what we want to be when we grow up; all the places we plan to visit someday.

"But it's only nine-thirty," Jeannine says.

"I said 'lights out,'" her mom says. "Not 'party's over!'" She comes in and hands us each a plastic flashlight before she turns off the overhead lights. "Why don't you pretend you're camping?" she says with a laugh. "I used to do that when I had sleepovers with my friends."

So we turn on our flashlights and pull the comforter over our heads.

"Did you ever go camping?" Jeannine asks us.

I shake my head.

"My grandparents have a trailer in New York. In the summer, we go there to visit," Solange says.

"That isn't real camping," Jeannine says. "Real camping is sleeping in a tent. And pooping in an outhouse." Which cracks Solange and me up.

I look up at the comforter overhead and at my friends' shining faces. "This feels kind of like a tent," I say.

"Maybe you two can come camping with us this summer," Jeannine says.

Her parents are watching a movie downstairs. Every once in a while we hear the sound of their laughter or the murmur of conversation.

I swallow a yawn. I don't want to fall asleep.

"I think I smell popcorn," Solange says.

Jeannine slips out from under the comforter and our tent collapses. She opens her bedroom door. "Are you guys having popcorn without us?" she hollers.

"We were just going to invite you to have some," Jeannine's dad calls back.

When we go downstairs, Jeannine's parents pause the movie. Her mom offers us some popcorn, and I take a handful—it's soaked in salty butter.

When Jeannine's mom's phone rings, she puts down the

popcorn bowl and goes to the kitchen to take the call.

I hear her say hello but then nothing else for a while. "Are you sure? They're having such a good time . . ." There's another pause and then Jeannine's mom says, "No, it's not a problem. I'll drive her back."

I'll drive her back?

It has to be my mom calling, not Solange's. I get up from the love seat where the three of us are sitting. Jeannine's mom is coming out of the kitchen at the same time I'm walking in. "Is something wrong at my house?" I ask her.

"Your mother has a migraine. She says she needs you to be there in the morning. For your little sister."

Shoot, shoot, shoot! Why did she have to get a migraine now—when I was having such a good day? But because I don't have a choice, I go upstairs and repack the overnight bag I packed this morning. Jeannine and Solange come too, but at first they don't say anything. They just watch as I pull a T-shirt over my pajamas. "I really wish I didn't have to go," I mutter.

"It won't be as much fun without you," Solange says. "Though there'll be more room in the bed."

"We'll have another sleepover soon," Jeannine promises.

I don't look at the bed that was our tent half an hour ago. It would hurt too much.

Jeannine's mom is also wearing a T-shirt over her pajamas.

"I'm sorry you have to drive me back," I say once we're in the car.

"It's not a problem, honey. Does she get a lot of headaches?" she asks.

"She used to."

Jeannine's mom doesn't mention Mom's headaches again. When we get to the condo, she parks in the driveway and insists on bringing me to the elevator. She's not worried about anyone seeing her in her pajamas.

In the lobby, she pats my arm. "I'm sure your mom will be okay, but if you need me for anything at all, just phone. It doesn't matter what time it is."

"Thanks," I say. "For everything."

The girl I see on the mirrored walls of the elevator looks lost and sad. Not just because her sleepover ended early. But also because of the way Jeannine's mom spoke to her—to *me*. As if she understood.

Mom meets me at the door. Her eyes have that glassy look again. "Thank God you're back," she says.

"Did you take something for the headache?" I ask her.

"I will now that you're here." She presses one hand to her forehead. The pain must be bad.

"You sleep in tomorrow. I'll take care of Bea."

"That's why I needed you home, Justine," she says.

I bring my overnight bag to my room. On the way, I stop to look in at Bea. One of her feet is sticking out from the bottom of her purple blanket. I pull the blanket so she's completely covered. She sighs in her sleep.

Mom doesn't leave her bed on Sunday except to go to the bathroom. When I ask if she wants me to bring her something to eat, she can barely whisper *no*.

I read Bea four chapter books—one of them twice. We do drawings together and I help her practice her letters. I make sure she gets three meals, and I don't leave any dishes afterward. After supper, I give her a bath and wash her hair. I supervise as she flosses and brushes her teeth.

By Sunday night, Mom is well enough to have a cup of tea—and phone Darlene.

I've been so busy taking care of Bea I haven't had time to think. It's only when I'm lying in bed that night that I realize Mom never asked about the sleepover. And she never said she was sorry for making me come home early. I shouldn't blame her for the first thing. A person with a migraine can't be expected to ask about a sleepover.

But even a person with a migraine could have thanked me for looking after Bea.

My new phone is safely hidden under my mattress. Just the thought of it cheers me up.

CHAPTER TWENTY-FIVE

The judge presiding over our case is a woman named Judge Twillings.

Mom thinks having a woman judge could help us. Maître Pépin thinks so too.

Mom explained that Judge Twillings has already made what's called a *ruling* in the case. "She has issued something called a temporary safeguard order," Mom tells Bea and me after school on Friday. "That means for the next four weeks, you'll be able to see your father—"

"Yay." Bea stands up and wiggles her butt. "And Sheldon too?"

I haven't had the heart to tell Bea about Sheldon.

"No," Mom tells Bea. "Sheldon can't come."

"Can't come where?" I ask Mom.

"I'm getting to that, Justine. When Maître Pépin told

Judge Twillings about the mold problem, she came up with a different plan."

"But I thought Dad found a mold expert," I say.

"He may have found one," Mom says, "but so far there's no report. And until there's a report, you can't go back to your father's house. It isn't safe, for all kinds of reasons."

"I miss Dad," Bea says. "And Sheldon. And Grandmami."

"I know you do, honeybee. But I haven't quite finished explaining things," Mom says. "For the next month, you two will be seeing your father every Saturday afternoon for forty-five minutes at a facility called The Midway."

Forty-five minutes isn't a lot, but it's better than nothing. I just hope it'll be enough to make Dad stop hurting. Because I can't forget what Mariella said about Dad. And I know it's my fault.

"Can't Sheldon come to The Mid?" Bea doesn't bother with the second syllable.

"Sheldon can't come. I looked into it already," Mom says.

"You did?" I thought Mom didn't approve of Sheldon.

"I did. I know how much you miss that cat. But The Midway has a strict no-pets rule," Mom explains.

"When's the hearing gonna be?" I ask Mom.

"*Going to* be," Mom says. "Not for at least four months. Unless it gets expedited."

"What's exp—?" Bea stumbles on the word.

Even I don't know what *expedited* means.

"Expedited means there would be some reason to advance the hearing—to speed things up." Mom pauses as if she is thinking. "For the time being, it doesn't look like that will happen."

So on Saturday after lunch, Mom drives us to The Midway. It's in the east end of Montreal—farther east even than the refineries and the old Molson Brewery—and we have to take the Jacques Cartier Bridge to get there. When we get off the highway, a squeegee kid runs up from the sidewalk and starts cleaning the windshield of Mom's car. She shoos him away, but when I look out the window at the boy's face, I get the feeling he isn't dangerous. He doesn't look that much older than me. So I take out the toonie in my wallet and ask Mom to give it to him.

"That's very generous of you," she says, meeting my eye in the rearview mirror. She rolls down the window to hand the boy the coin. "It's from my daughter," she tells him. Then she adds, "Be careful out here in the traffic, okay?" Mom rolls the window back up.

The boy looks into the back seat where I am sitting. "Thanks." He mouths the word before the light turns green and he has to hurry back to the sidewalk.

Bea turns to look at me. "Why did you give him money?" she wants to know.

"Because he lives on the street," I tell her.

"Justine," Mom says. I hear the warning in her voice. I guess she doesn't want Bea thinking about street people. "I don't know what I'm going to do with myself for forty-five minutes in *this* neighborhood," she says as she drives up to the small gray building.

"You can have coffee," Bea tells Mom. "See, there's a Tim Hortons!"

"Life's too short for Tim Hortons coffee," Mom mutters. "I'll read in the car. With the doors locked."

Next door to The Midway are two boarded-up buildings, and on the other side, a tattoo parlor.

Mom parks the car in front of The Midway and walks us to the door. "Are you coming inside?" Bea asks her.

Mom shakes her head. "I'm supposed to leave you at the front door. But when you come out, I'll be waiting in the car." Mom gives us each a peck on the cheek. "You two are my keel. I don't know how I'd stay afloat without you."

"What's a keel?" Bea asks.

"It's a part of a boat, honeybee," Mom tells her.

"Hey, is that why when people are tired or stressed out, they say they're going to keel over?" I ask Mom.

"Hmm," Mom says. "I never thought of that. It's the same word. Just a different way of using it."

"You're not going to keel over, are you, Mom?" I ask her.

"Not as long as I have you two," she says. She kisses both of our foreheads before she heads back to the car.

Bea reaches for my hand. She doesn't do that so much anymore. Lately, she's been acting more grown-up. Maybe something about coming to The Midway makes her feel littler. I squeeze her hand.

She tugs on my sleeve. "Who's Daddy's keel?"

I look at Bea. That's a seriously smart question for a four-year-old. I know she expects an answer. "Mariella's his keel. And Grandmami."

I wonder if Bea noticed I didn't mention Sheldon. Maybe if enough time goes by, Bea will forget all about Sheldon. But who am I kidding? That'll never happen. Bea loves that cat. And I do too. If only there was something I could do to help find a family to adopt him. Maybe I can put ads on the bulletin board at school and at the grocery store. Should I mention that he only has one eye?

There's a woman security guard standing inside the front entrance of The Midway, and I spot two round mirrors near the ceiling. The security guard nods at us. Somebody buzzes us in. When we walk inside, a woman speaks to us from behind a hard plastic window. "Good morning, ladies. Names please." Her cheerful voice sounds out of place here.

"Justine and Bea Tepper," I say.

"I can tell her my own name," Bea says. "It's Beatrice."

"Third door to the right," the woman tells us. "Your father is already here."

Something about this place reminds me of the SPCA. It could be the gray walls, or the smell of cleaning products. Whoever's in charge should spruce it up. I check for a bulletin board where I could post a sign about Sheldon, but there isn't one. The walls are completely bare.

The third door to the right is open. We pass two other closed doors on our way there. Behind one, I hear hushed voices. Behind the other, I hear someone sobbing. Something in my chest tightens. I'm remembering all the cats at the SPCA. I really hope we can find a good home for Sheldon. Everyone needs a family to love them, even a cat.

We see Dad before he sees us. He is sitting at a white table, reading the paper.

"Daddy!" Bea squeals.

Dad drops the newspaper. Before he can get up from his chair, Bea tackles him. "Daddy! Daddy! Daddy!" she says over and over again. "Daddy! Daddy! Daddy! I love you, Daddy."

"I love you too, honeybee." Dad's voice sounds gravelly.

There is a young guy sitting at the table too, checking something on his phone. For a second I wonder who he is, then I realize this must be what *supervised visits* means. He's a supervisor. His job is to make sure dads behave. And maybe some moms too.

Behind the table is a gray metal shelf with kids' books and some board games. That must be to keep kids busy if they run out of stuff to talk about with their dads—or moms. We won't need the books or games because we always have something to talk about with Dad.

I get that tight feeling again in my chest. All this—The Midway and its bare gray walls; Mom reading in her car; Dad sitting at the table with some supervisor—is my fault. I never told Fred that Dad didn't mean to hurt Bea.

I push that thought away.

I said what I said because I had to. For Mom. Because we're her keel. I look over at Bea, who has pulled over a chair so close to Dad's that the two chairs are touching. I did it for us. But especially for Mom. So she doesn't keel over.

"Hiya, Dad," I say quietly.

When I take a seat at the table, the supervisor gets up from his chair. He tucks his phone into his back pocket. "My name's Jeffrey," he says. "I'll be supervising your visit today." Then he sits back down at the end of the table.

Dad sucks in his lips. I do that too when I am trying not to say something that could get me into trouble. Jeffrey points to a clock on the wall behind us. "You guys have forty-five minutes."

"So how are you two girls doing?" Dad's voice sounds stiff, like he's an actor practicing his lines. His posture's weird too. He's trying not to slump. He doesn't like being supervised. Neither do I.

When I look at Jeffrey, he gives me the world's tiniest nod. We're supposed to pretend he's not here—only it's hard to pretend that someone sitting at the same table isn't there.

Bea turns to Jeffrey. "Do you have to sit so close to us?" she asks him.

I cover my mouth so Jeffrey won't hear me laugh.

Jeffrey's face reddens. "Uh," he says. "I usually sit at the table with clients. But I could move away. If you want me to."

Dad clears his throat. "We want you to."

Jeffrey moves his chair closer to the wall. "I realize this can be awkward at first. But after one or two visits, most clients forget I'm here."

"We're good, Dad," I tell him. "Busy with school. The usual." Then because it's true, I add, "We miss you."

"I had a stuffy nose." Bea makes it sound like national news. "But it went away. How 'bout you, Daddy? How's Sheldon?"

"I'm . . . you know . . . okay." Dad looks down at his feet. "Sheldon's okay too."

Bea bows her head. "I miss Sheldon. And Marry. And Grandmami."

"I know," Dad tells her. "So what have you two been learning at school?" I'm glad he changed the subject.

"In English, we're learning how to write the three-paragraph essay." I say it brightly because I want to change up the mood in this sad gray room. "Mr. Farber says each paragraph is like a car on a train, and the cars need to be attached. Solange says her essays are train wrecks."

I hoped Dad would laugh at Solange's joke, but he just nods as if I said something very interesting.

Her chair must not have been close enough to Dad's, because Bea has gone to sit on his lap. "We learned a new song," she says, bopping. "It's Spanish. D'you want me to sing it?" She closes her eyes and starts singing before Dad can say yes.

"*Arrorró mi niño, arrorró mi sol, arrorró pedazo, de mi corazón* . . . Do you know what it means, Daddy? I do! And I'm only four!"

When I look at Dad, I see he is tearing up and using the back of his hand to wipe his eyes. Crying can't be a good idea during supervised visits, but Jeffrey doesn't say anything.

Bea is too excited about her song to notice that Dad is getting emotional. "It means, 'Go to sleep my baby, go to sleep my sun.' And the ending means, 'You're a piece of my heart.'" When Dad sniffles, Bea turns to face him. "Daddy, you okay?" She pats his shoulder. Something about the way she does it makes me feel sadder than sad.

Dad's Adam's apple jiggles. "I'm okay," he says, though he doesn't sound okay at all. "You two girls are a piece of my heart. That's why this"—Dad looks around the small room—"is so hard. I don't know why she did this to me."

I gulp. He means Mom. But I'm the one who did this to him. Not her.

Jeffrey gets up from his chair. "Sir, it's better if you don't go there."

"Go where?" Bea asks. "Daddy isn't going anywhere. We're stuck here. With you."

Supervisors may not be allowed to laugh, but Jeffrey does. After that, it's easier to forget he's in the room. We tell Dad more about school. He tells us how when he tried to make homemade pizza, the dough ended up on the ceiling and he had to stand on a ladder to get it off.

"It's good Mom wasn't there. She doesn't like messes," Bea says.

"Your grandmother didn't like it very much either,"

Dad says. "She insisted on sitting on the bottom rung so the ladder wouldn't crash." I can just picture Grandmami sitting there, telling Dad to be careful and calling him her little boy. And Dad telling her to cut it out.

When our time is up, Jeffrey explains that we have to leave before Dad. Whoever runs The Midway must not want parents who don't get along meeting up in the lobby or the parking lot.

"See you next week, Daddy," Bea tells Dad.

I give Dad a hug. He squeezes me hard, and I nearly start to cry. I feel sad and guilty at the same time. I made all this happen. Dad squeezes me harder. Which only makes me feel worse.

Jeffrey leads me and Bea out of the room. Something makes me turn around to give Dad one last look. He's hunched at the table, holding his head between his hands.

CHAPTER TWENTY-SIX

Saturday, Oct. 27

I don't know what you are exactly, Pink Notebook. I know what you were. But I don't need that anymore. What I need right now is a place to say how I feel. Because I've got a lot of feelings. And if I don't let them out, well . . . I'm afraid I might be the one to explode.

One of Mom's African violets has never bloomed. The others get small bright-pink or deep-purple flowers. But that one violet only ever has green furry leaves. I always feel sorry for that plant.

Today, I noticed the teensiest bud on it. It was mostly green, but with a touch of light pink in the middle, just like you, Pink Notebook. Seeing that light pink made me feel the tiniest bit better.

Does everyone who keeps a journal always reread what they just wrote? Or is it just me?

Whenever I used to reread my notes about Dad, I always felt proud for being so observant and because I knew I was helping Mom.

But rereading what I just wrote feels different.

It feels uncomfortable.

Maybe being a flower bud is uncomfortable too. You're about to change, but you don't know what's coming next.

I tear out the two entries from the back of my notebook. They don't belong. But something stops me from throwing them away.

I don't want to forget what uncomfortable feels like.

ooo

Mom's been sitting us down a lot lately. This time we're not in the kitchen, where she usually makes important announcements. We're at Baker's Dozen, a doughnut shop and café near the condo. We don't come here often because Mom says it's an unnecessary splurge. As soon as she mentions the words *Baker's Dozen*, I know whatever Mom has to tell us must be big news. Only it's bigger than I expected.

The barista made a heart in the foam on Mom's soy milk

latté. Now Mom uses the back of her coffee spoon to make the heart go away.

She let me order a doughnut with pink icing and sprinkles. Of course, Bea copied me.

Bea takes a too-big bite of doughnut. Some pink and blue sprinkles get stuck to her lips and she licks them off. "Is it about the *super* visits?" she asks.

"Bea, darling," Mom says. "Try to remember that you have to wait to speak until there's no food left in your mouth."

Bea puts her hand over her mouth. "Oops," she says.

Mom takes a sip of coffee, then rests her palms on the table and looks up at us. "All right, here goes," she says. "I'm thinking of taking a job in Ottawa. It's a very good job—a promotion—with another advertising agency."

Ottawa? That's like a hundred miles away. In another province. She's got to be kidding! Except Mom doesn't kid around.

The doughnut isn't sitting right in my stomach. "Ottawa's really far. How are you gonna—I mean, *going to* —drive there and back five days a week?" I ask.

For a second, Mom looks confused. "I won't be driving back and forth." She pauses. "We're moving to Ottawa. Of course, we'll need Judge Twillings's permission." She smiles and reaches out to squeeze our hands as if this is the best news ever, and I won't have to go to a brand-new school and make brand-new friends all over again.

"When?" I ask. "And what about the condo?" I know how attached she is to the condo.

"Soon," Mom says. "I'm hoping to start the second week of January. We'll rent out the condo, and put it up for sale in the spring. Winter isn't a good time to sell a condo in this city. Not with all the snow and ice."

"What about Daddy—and Sheldon?" Bea asks.

Mom makes a steeple with her hands. "I'm coming to that. Judge Twillings has agreed to expedite the hearing. Remember how I told you that *expedite* means to speed things up? Well, that's what Judge Twillings did. All because of this wonderful job offer. You'll still be able to see your father..." Mom pauses. "And Sheldon several times a year. Just not every weekend, of course."

"Will it be super—" Bea starts to ask.

"We don't know that part yet. That's up to Judge Twillings. She'll decide what's best."

A hard lump starts to form in my throat. I know that unless she finds some way for us to spend more time with her, Mom'll never stop worrying. But I never dreamed she'd make us move to another city! What about Solange and Jeannine? How will I ever make friends like them again? This isn't right! Mom should've talked to us first, or at least warned us this could happen. You can't just go announcing something like this to your kids at a doughnut shop! Why didn't she think of us—or at least ask for our opinion?

By planning this move without us, Mom is acting like Benito Mussolini. (We had to learn a whole list of dictators for school last year, but Benito is the one I remember.)

"I don't like Ottawa," I mutter under my breath. "I like Montreal." I don't mutter this time. "I also like democracy."

"Me too," Bea whispers. I don't know whether Bea is saying she likes Montreal or democracy. I doubt she even knows what democracy means.

Mom doesn't want to discuss democracy. She waves her hand through the air. I bet Benito did that too. "You hardly know Ottawa, girls. We've only been there once or twice for a day at a time. It's a lovely city with a canal for skating, and a tulip festival in the spring. And don't forget, it's our nation's capital."

Our nation's capital? Give me a break! Does Mom really think that's a selling point?

Bea hangs her head. "I don't like tulips," she says. "I like roses. Tulips don't have a smell."

Mom gently strokes the top of Bea's hand. "I know this

is hard for you, honeybee, and for your sister too." Her eyes meet mine when she says that. "But we don't have a choice."

"*We?*" I ask. Moving to Ottawa isn't about *us*. It's about her!

Mom raises her eyebrows as if she's surprised I said that. "Yes, *we*," she answers calmly. "It's always *we*, Justine. We can't let the situation drag on. Accepting this job is our only way to speed things up."

Bea has forgotten all about what's left of her doughnut. "What about Daddy?" she asks again. "And Marry?" Bea's voice breaks. "And Sheldon?"

Bea's right. I've been thinking so much about how I'll miss my friends I haven't really thought about what it would feel like to live in a different city from Dad and Mariella. How often will we get to see them? Ottawa's not that close. I know for sure Mom will never drive us all the way to Montreal on snowy weekends—and we get a lot of those in winter.

"I told you, Bea," Mom says. "You'll get to see all of them. Just a little less often."

A little less often? What does that mean exactly? I know Mom well enough to know that if she's being vague, she's doing it on purpose. She knows how many weekends we'll get to spend with Dad; she just doesn't want to tell us.

"Not Sheldon," I blurt out. "She won't get to see Sheldon."

Bea makes a strange whimpering sound.

I shouldn't have said that about Sheldon. It's just that I'm upset. Upset and confused and fed up. But now I've gone and made Bea even sadder.

Mom sucks in her breath and shakes her head as if to say she can't take much more. When she does that, my old worry comes back—what if she falls apart again? Then what? "Is there something wrong with Sheldon?" Mom asks me.

Bea's eyes tear up. Even though I wish I could, I can't undo what I said. "Is Sheldon gonna die?" Bea asks in a tiny voice.

"There's nothing wrong with Sheldon," I tell her. "It's Mariella. She found out she has a cat allergy. A serious cat allergy. Daddy has to get r—" I stop myself from saying *get rid of him*. "He has to find Sheldon another home."

Mom takes a long sip of her latté. "I know you care for him," she tells Bea. "But we can't base our plans on some cat."

"Mom!"

Mom raises her eyebrow. "Why are you *Mom*-ing me, Justine?"

"Because sometimes I wonder if you even have a heart." I can't take those words back. But right now, I don't want to.

Mom's eyes flash. Is this the first time in all my life I've ever talked back to her? I've thought about doing it before, but something always stops me. *Mom has so much on her shoulders. Mom tries so hard. Mom is fragile. Mom needs my help. Mom has anxiety.* But right now, none of that matters.

Mom raises her hand in the air again. It looks like she wants to slap me. Not that she's ever done that. But I've never talked back to her before.

She looks at her hand as if it's something strange, like a UFO, and lets it fall back on the table. She doesn't reprimand me for being rude. Her face is pale and she looks stressed out. "One day," she says quietly, "you'll understand the sacrifices I've made for the two of you."

I sigh. There's no point arguing. I know this is all about expediting the hearing. Not about all the sacrifices she's made.

Besides, Mom always wins.

Which means that as long as Judge Twillings gives Mom permission, Bea and I are moving to Ottawa. Even if we don't want to.

"Could we take Sheldon?" Bea asks in that same tiny voice. "Please . . . could we? You said we might get a cat of our own one day!"

Mom sighs. "Today isn't that day, honeybee. Besides, Sheldon is not our problem."

At least this time Mom called Sheldon by his name.

CHAPTER TWENTY-SEVEN

I can't sleep. Counting sheep isn't working. I flip onto my other side. Mariella's trick when she can't sleep is turning her pillow over. She says it always works. But it doesn't work for me. It only reminds me that if we move to Ottawa, I'll hardly ever get to see my big sister.

I reach under the mattress for my phone and send Mariella a text. *Miss you. Can't sleep.* I look at the screen for fifteen minutes, but Mariella doesn't text me back. She must be sound asleep. For a moment, I wonder what it would feel like if Leonor was my mother too. I wouldn't mind the Portuguese accent, and I'd get to eat *natas* all the time. Leonor doesn't worry about sugar. And she and Dad get along. They even try to help each other. Like when Dad picks up stuff for her at Costco because she isn't a member.

I can't stop thinking about Ottawa, and Dad and

Mariella and Sheldon, and how Solange and Jeannine will forget they ever knew me. That's what happens when you don't see people. They forget you.

I feel a cramp in my stomach when I picture myself walking into a new classroom at some new school. All the other kids' eyes are on me—checking me out as the teacher announces my name. Then she asks, "Who'd like to volunteer to be Justine's buddy?" Her voice is friendly, but nobody raises their hand. If I could turn into a puddle, I would.

Thinking of puddles makes me thirsty. Maybe if I have some water, I'll be able to forget my complicated life and fall asleep.

Bea's door is slightly open, and because the hallway light is on, I can see her sleeping, and hear her quiet snore. How come Bea can sleep?

There's a sliver of yellow light underneath Mom's door. She must be up too. If things were different—if she wasn't acting like Mussolini—I might knock on her door. Maybe I'd crawl into her bed the way I did when I was little. Maybe I'd snuggle with her until I dozed off. Then she'd carry me back to my bed, the way she still does with Bea when Bea falls asleep in the den.

When I get to the kitchen, I pour myself a glass of water from the pitcher on the counter. I take a sip and gaze out the window. The sky is full of stars, and far below me, in the distance, I see car lights twinkling past. What are all those people doing out this late? Coming home from a party, or just finishing a night shift at work? They're all grown-ups, of course. Being grown-up means having a lot to worry about—why else are adults always saying they wish they could be kids again? But at least they get to make their own decisions. That's the part I'm looking forward to. I've had it with adults making decisions for me.

It's only when I'm coming back from the kitchen with my glass of water that I realize Mom is on the phone.

She must be talking to Darlene. Who else would she be talking to in the middle of the night? Why doesn't Mom have other friends? One friend's not enough. Maybe it's not because Mom's busy with us, or because she'd rather not spend money on going out for lunch with people from work. Maybe it's because she's sometimes hard to get along with.

Something—I'm not sure what—makes me stand outside her door and listen. She'd freak if she knew. But she doesn't know, and she's not going to find out.

"He does sound like a nice man," I hear Mom say. "But, Dar, I'm warning you. Proceed with caution. You never know with men. Remember how crazy I was about Alain at first... and then, well, we all know how that went."

Does Darlene have a boyfriend? In all the years we've

known her she's never had one. I wonder if Will knows, and if he does, what he thinks of the guy.

Mom doesn't say anything. Maybe she's hung up, but then I hear her say, "You need to be especially careful when you meet someone online."

I can't picture Darlene doing online dating, but that must be how she met the guy. "Maybe," I hear Mom say. "Maybe once we've settled in, in Ottawa. Though I'd prefer if it happened in real life."

As if my life isn't already messed up enough! What if Mom meets some guy in real life—or on some dating website? What if he's a doofus? What if I hate him? Then what? What about Dad? He's already had two wives. Maybe he wants a third. Maybe the woman will have kids of her own.

All this could happen one day. One of them—maybe both of them—could fall in love, and I'd end up with a stepmother or stepfather, and possibly stepsiblings.

I don't understand why my life has to keep changing all the time. Why can't things ever just stay the same, at least for a while? Or at least long enough for me to get used to them? It's hard enough having to wake up in two different houses, but right now that doesn't seem so bad.

I'm about to head back to my room, though I've decided I'm never going to be able to fall asleep again. (It was bad enough picturing myself, a total reject at some new school—but now I have to picture Mom or Dad with a new partner and my evil, annoying, bathroom-hogging stepsiblings.)

But something I hear Mom say—and the way she says it—makes me forget all about these worries.

"I'm going to have to tell the judge I'm prepared to move to Ottawa without the girls."

Without us?

What does that mean?

I have to stop myself from marching into Mom's room. Without us? *You're going to tell the judge you'd move to Ottawa* without us? *The thing that worried you most was our spending too much time with Dad! If you went to Ottawa without us, we'd end up living with him!*

Even more than not wanting to move to Ottawa, I don't want Mom to leave us with Dad. I don't want her abandoning us. Because that's the right word for what she's talking about. *Abandoning* her daughters.

"Not that I'd want to," I hear Mom add.

My body relaxes, but only a little.

"But Maître Pépin says it's what I have to tell Judge Twillings," Mom continues. "Otherwise, she'd never have agreed to expedite the case in the first place. Maître Pépin says that if, when I'm in court, the judge asks whether I'm prepared to move without them, I have to say yes. It's the only way I can show her that I'm serious about the job. And to be honest, Dar, sometimes I feel as if I just need to get away from this whole situation."

Darlene is saying something, but I can't make out the words. I know she's raised her voice, because how else could I hear her through the door?

"Don't talk to me like that!" I hear Mom snap.

But Darlene keeps talking.

"You don't understand," Mom says. "Maître Pépin made it clear that I don't have a choice. A real friend would never say those things."

Darlene's not finished. I can still hear her voice.

In the middle of a sentence, her voice stops. Mom has ended the call. "I don't need you," I hear Mom say. But then she makes a strange gulping sound.

My head hurts from trying to make sense of what I just heard.

Judge Twillings will only let Mom take us with her to Ottawa if she says she'd be willing to leave us behind?

I'm starting to hate Judge Twillings.

CHAPTER TWENTY-EIGHT

Mom had to be in court first thing today. She explained how she and Dad, their lawyers and Fred would probably be in Judge Twillings's courtroom all morning. I don't testify until this afternoon. That's why Darlene will be picking me up at school.

"I thought you and Dar—" I stopped myself. I didn't want Mom to know I'd overheard their conversation the other night. "Everything okay with Darlene?" I asked instead.

Mom gave me a funny look. "Why would you ask me that?"

"No reason."

She rubbed her forehead. "There have been times," she said, "when Darlene and I haven't always seen eye to eye. The two of us had a little squabble the other night."

I couldn't believe Mom was telling me all that. "You did?" I tried to sound surprised. "I guess if she's coming to pick me up at school it means you two must've fixed things, right?"

"I don't know if things are fixed. But I do know one thing—Darlene loves you and Bea. That's why she's picking you up. And why she's planning to spend the afternoon at the courthouse. So you won't have to be alone."

ooo

Darlene is parked in front of my school at lunchtime. "Hi, sweetheart," she says when I get into her car. "How you doing?"

Something about the way she says it makes me want to cry.

How *am* I doing?

I don't know.

"Okay, I guess," I say.

I wish I could ask Darlene about what I heard Mom tell her about going to Ottawa without us. But I decide it's better not to. Darlene hums as we cross the Champlain Bridge and head toward downtown. Usually when people hum, their lips are slightly loose. Darlene's are pursed together in a way that makes me think she's holding something in too.

I look out the window at the blue-black water beneath us and think about Judge Twillings and pray she doesn't ask Mom if she'd move without us. Because what if Mom says yes, and Judge Twillings decides Bea and I should live with Dad? Then what? I try telling myself that'll never happen. Judges don't take kids away from their mothers unless their mothers are really bad—drink too much or do drugs or beat their kids. My mom would never do anything like that.

I check the clock on the dashboard. It's 12:35. By now, Judge Twillings will have heard what a terrible job Dad does taking care of Bea and me.

I take a deep breath. "Bea's too young to testify in court," I say to Darlene. "But I'm old enough." Saying those words makes me proud and nervous at the same time. My testimony is super important. Judge Twillings will be listening carefully to every word I say.

Without lifting her eyes from the road, Darlene reaches out to pat my hand. "I know," she says quietly. "You're a very brave girl, Justine. I admire you."

My eyes fill up with tears, but I don't cry. No one's ever told me before that they think I'm brave or that they admire me. And Darlene's not the sort of person who throws compliments around like confetti. She wouldn't say those things if she didn't mean them. I hope she's right. That I really am brave and admirable.

Darlene parks in a giant lot across from the courthouse. It's almost full. I didn't realize so many other families had legal problems too. It makes me sad for all of them, especially the kids.

I'm about to open the car door when Darlene stops me. "Jus . . . tine." The way she breaks my name into two syllables makes me think she isn't sure whether she should go on.

"Yes?"

"This may not be my place. But here's the thing. Will told me about the Wi-Fi password. It isn't right. Your mother's still very angry with your dad. I've told her she shouldn't be dragging you into her battle. You need to be your own person, honey. You're not somebody's soldier."

I bite my lip. "I'll try," I tell her.

"Okay, then," Darlene says. "And hey, Justine . . . just so you know, I adore you."

"I adore you too," I mumble, though I'm pretty sure Darlene wouldn't adore me so much if she knew what I'd done.

Darlene holds my hand as we walk toward the courthouse. It's just an ordinary office building with black windows and white walls. Pretty much anything could be going on inside a building like this.

Darlene pulls open the black glass double door and we go inside. A security guard checks Darlene's purse, then my backpack. When he hands her purse back, she remembers that she has something for me. "Will made you a card."

"He *made* me a card?" Will isn't exactly artsy.

Darlene hands me a square white envelope with my name on it. "He made it on the computer. That still counts."

I tuck the envelope under my arm. Just having it there makes me feel better. Will knows pretty much everything about me—and my family. Maybe one day, when all this is over, I'll be able to tell Jeannine and Solange about it too.

I don't expect the guard to spend so long looking inside my backpack—do I look like someone who might have a weapon? He even takes out my pink notebook. For a second, I worry he might start reading it, but then he stuffs it back in my bag.

Darlene eyes my notebook. She must like the pink cover and the silver stars. "Writing's a good outlet for you," she says. "When I was your age, I kept a journal too. It helped me figure out who I was in the world. Sometimes I think I should take up journal writing again."

At the information desk by the escalator, Darlene tells the clerk my last name. She scrolls down her computer screen. "You're on the second floor. Two-point-two-four. Family court," she says, without looking up from her computer.

You wouldn't expect bad things to happen in a place called *family court*. They should call it what it really is: *custody battle court*.

We head for the escalator. My shoulders stiffen when, up ahead, I see a man flanked by two security guards. What did he do to end up between those guys?

Darlene catches my elbow to make me stop walking. She doesn't want for us to be on the escalator at the same time as the man. When we reach the second floor, I spot him again. This time I see his face. I don't know what I expected, but he looks ordinary—he has pale skin, a thin nose, tired eyes. Not like a criminal. Can you tell from someone's face if he's done bad stuff? For a millisecond, our eyes meet, and I get the feeling he knows what I'm thinking. Then he looks away.

"Justine," Darlene is telling me, "it's to the left."

I head for Room 2.24, but Darlene takes my arm and leads me to a bench down the corridor. "We're supposed to wait outside till it's your turn to testify. Your lawyer will come out to get you."

Even the corridor here feels sad and serious. It reminds me of when I went to the funeral home after Jeannine's grandmother died.

Darlene must sense I don't feel like talking. She takes her cellphone out and smiles as she reads a text. "Is it from your boyfriend?" I ask her. "The guy you met online?"

Darlene turns to look at me. "How do you know about that?"

I don't want to admit I was eavesdropping. "Uh, I just guessed."

Darlene laughs. "He's not my boyfriend. We're just getting to know each other. But you know? He's nice."

Darlene puts her phone away and takes a sudoku puzzle book out of her purse. I rest my head on her shoulder as she starts the puzzle.

Then I remember Will's card. Darlene hears me tear open the envelope, but she doesn't look up from her sudoku. If it was Mom, she'd be reading over my shoulder.

There's a photo of me on the front. I can't be much older than Bea is now, and I'm flexing one arm. The picture makes me laugh. I open the card. The font is so big Will's three-word message takes up most of the inside:

You got this.

I hope Will's right.

I don't know how much time passes before the door to Room 2.24 finally opens.

Someone's coming out. Someone dressed in a black cape that makes him look like Dracula. It's the red Converse high-tops that give him away. Fred.

He waves as he comes over. Underneath the cape, he's

wearing black pants and a long-sleeved white shirt. He must be trying to hide his dragon tattoo.

I introduce him and Darlene. "Darlene's my mom's best friend," I tell Fred. "Most days anyhow. This is Fred," I tell Darlene. "My lawyer." Saying that makes me feel very grown-up.

"Thanks for being here," Fred tells Darlene. "I heard you drove in from the Townships."

"That's what friends are for," Darlene says. "You know what they say—good friendships last longer than most marriages."

"I never heard that. But I get it. People are lucky when they have good friends." Fred leans down and looks into my eyes. "It's nearly time for you to testify, Justine. Let's just give your parents a few minutes to leave the courtroom first."

Mom and Dad won't be there when I testify. It'll just be me, the three lawyers, Judge Twillings, a clerk and someone called a stenographer who takes notes. Like me, I guess.

It's weird to see my parents leaving the courtroom at the same time. Mom and Maître Pépin walk out first; Dad and his lawyer, who's a woman, are behind them. Maybe Judge Twillings warned them not to look at me, because none of them do. They head the opposite way and for a minute, I wonder if they're all going to share a bench. Which would be even weirder.

"Okay," Fred says. "You got this, Justine?"

The same words Will wrote in his card. Only Fred turned them into a question. I think about that old photo of me, flexing my muscles.

"I think so."

"All you need to do is be yourself."

I nod, but when Fred adds, "And tell the truth," something makes me look away.

CHAPTER TWENTY-NINE

Nothing is turning out like I expected.

The courtroom looks more like a classroom than someplace official. All that's missing is a whiteboard. There are rows of chairs on either side, facing a raised platform with a black desk, and next to it is what must be the witness box.

There's no sign of Judge Twillings. Maybe she's in the bathroom. Even judges sometimes have to pee.

There are three more desks near the front of the room. Maître Pépin sits down at the one that is farthest away. Dad's lawyer takes the desk on the other end. Though I hear Maître Pépin's name a lot, I realize now that Dad has never mentioned his lawyer to us. I don't even know her name.

Everyone stands up when a side door opens and Judge Twillings walks in. She sits down behind the tall desk on the platform. She has short curly hair and funky red glasses.

I wish I could ask her to be in a selfie with me, but it's probably illegal for judges to be in photos. Except maybe on weekends when they're with their families.

Judge Twillings smiles at me. It's the kind of smile the crossing guard gives you the first day of school. A smile that says, *I look forward to keeping you safe all year.* Are judges even allowed to smile like that?

Fred brings me to the witness stand. "There's a glass of water if you need it," he tells me before he returns to his desk, exactly halfway between the other two lawyers' desks. I wonder if that's on purpose.

"Good afternoon, Justine. You need to take an oath before we begin," Judge Twillings explains. "Clerk." Judge Twillings turns to a woman standing at the side of the courtroom. The woman, who is dressed all in black, steps forward.

"Aren't you supposed to have a Bible?" I ask her.

Judge Twillings answers for the clerk. "In the province of Quebec, witnesses no longer swear on the Bible. You may proceed, Clerk."

"Please raise your right hand," the clerk instructs me. I raise my hand. "Now repeat after me. 'I solemnly affirm to tell the truth.'"

I take a small breath. *You got this,* I remind myself. *You need to do what you've been planning all along. For Mom.* "I solemnly affirm to tell the truth."

The courtroom is so quiet it's spooky. Who goes first? It turns out to be Judge Twillings. "Justine," she says, "I want to thank you for agreeing to testify today. It takes courage—even for grown-ups—to testify in a court of law. Because I want you to feel as comfortable as possible in my courtroom, I'd like to begin by asking you a few questions about yourself. Are you okay with that?"

This also isn't what I expected. What does Judge Twillings want to know about me? But I can't exactly ask her that. I swallow. "Sure."

"Please begin by telling us your full name."

Technically, it's not a question. Because if you wrote it out, you wouldn't need a question mark. It's what Mr. Farber told us is called an imperative statement. "Justine Tepper."

Judge Twillings peers at me through her red-rimmed glasses. Even her eyes are friendly. "Can you tell the court how old you are, Justine?"

Okay, that was a question. "Twelve."

"And what school you go to."

"Applewood Elementary. I'm in grade six. Oops, you didn't ask me that yet."

Judge Twillings adjusts her glasses. "You beat me to it,

Justine. I notice you didn't use your father's last name when I asked you to tell the court your name."

"I prefer to use only my mother's name." It's hard to do, but I look right at Judge Twillings. I want her to understand that what I just said matters.

Judge Twillings nods and says, "I see." That makes me feel better. She turns to Fred. "Maître Loisel, I understand you are representing both Justine and her sister, Beatrice, who is four years old. Are you ready to proceed?"

"Yes, Your Honor," says Fred. "Both girls have expressed their desire that their father's access be curtailed. The girls have told me they feel unsafe in their father's care."

I get a pang in my chest when Fred says that. I know it's a lie. But I can't think about that now. I just need to make sure Mom gets what she wants. And that she won't have to move to Ottawa to get what she wants.

"I see," Judge Twillings says. She says "I see" a lot. Maybe it's something she learned in judges' school. She turns back to me. "Justine." I brace myself because I'm pretty sure she's about to ask me something important, maybe even a question that will decide whatever happens here today. "Justine," Judge Twillings says again. "How are you doing?"

Why does everyone keep asking me that?

"Uh, uh, okay. I guess." Thank goodness I don't get choked

up this time. I hope it's all right that I have a question for Judge Twillings. "Did Fred . . . I mean, Maître Loisel . . . show you the pages he photocopied from my notebook?" Even just talking about my notebook makes me feel more confident.

"Your notebook?" Judge Twillings's glasses slip down her nose, but she doesn't bother adjusting them. I can tell she's curious.

"I was coming to that," Fred says, tapping his turquoise file folder. Fred takes the photocopied pages out of the folder and lays them on the judge's desk. "Justine has been keeping a detailed record of—" Fred pauses to look at Judge Twillings.

"Of what?" she asks.

"Of everything her father does wrong."

I sit up tall. Judge Twillings will be impressed when she sees the photocopied pages. "I brought the real book with me," I say, reaching down to the floor for my backpack. "In case you don't like photocopies."

"I see." Judge Twillings looks at me again. This time I feel like some rare bird she's spotted in the wild. "Do you also record the bad things your mother does?"

"No," I answer.

"Why not?" I can tell from the way she asks that she really is confused.

"Because"—I take a quick breath—"she doesn't do

anything bad." I mean to say the words calmly, but that isn't how they come out. They come out more like a sob. Maybe it's because of the pictures I'm seeing in my head. Mom blaming me for the spilled coffee on her bed. Mom getting angry with me about not buckling Bea into her car seat. Mom making me come back from the sleepover early. And then there's the picture I see of me: afraid of talking back to her, feeling like I always have to fix everything.

What was it Darlene said? *You're not somebody's soldier. You got this.*

I'm not somebody's soldier.

Not anymore.

I got this.

Judge Twillings doesn't say "I see" this time. Instead, she asks me for my notebook.

I hand it to the clerk, who hands it to the judge.

All I can tell from Judge Twillings's face while she reads is that she's concentrating. I watch her eyes move across the pages. She spends longer on one page; I think she's reading it twice. "I just read your account of the violent episode, Justine," she says. "According to what you've written here, your father's attack on Beatrice was unprovoked." Judge Twillings looks into my eyes. "Meaning there was no good reason for it."

I look back at her. I want to say something, but I can't find the right words.

Judge Twillings keeps talking. "Earlier today, your parents and their lawyers discussed that incident. Your father claims Beatrice ran across the street by herself, that she was chasing the family cat. Is it possible you left something out in your notes?" she asks.

She doesn't sound angry. She sounds sad. Like she feels sorry for me.

Why would she feel sorry for me?

As soon as I ask myself the question, I start to figure out the answer.

It's because Judge Twillings thinks I haven't been my own person.

Judge Twillings flips through the rest of my notebook, then looks back over at me. "Some pages seem to be missing from the back of this book. Was there anything special in those pages, Justine?"

I took an oath to tell the truth.

So this time, I do.

"I tried to write about my feelings," I tell Judge Twillings. "I didn't think you'd want to see that part."

Judge Twillings peers at me. "Your feelings matter," she says.

"I should have added the part about the cat. And about Bea crossing by herself."

"Thank you, Justine," Judge Twillings says. "I know you've been through a lot. Is there anything else you'd like to tell the court?"

She waits.

The three lawyers wait.

The courtroom is so quiet I can hear someone's watch ticking.

"I'm sorry. I made a mistake." It's not easy for me to get the words out, but I really need Judge Twillings and the lawyers to know.

The judge turns to me. "There's no need to apologize. You've been very helpful and very brave. We all make mistakes. The important thing is to learn from them. I understand there's someone waiting for you in the corridor. You can go back to her now."

Judge Twillings looks at the three lawyers. "I need to see the parents again."

CHAPTER THIRTY

I'm glad Darlene doesn't ask how things went. Because I have no idea. I never expected what just happened in the courtroom.

Darlene throws one arm around my shoulders. She's put away her puzzle book and is checking the news on her phone.

I have a crick in my neck. Probably from stress. But I'm not as stressed as before. At least now I've told the truth.

"There's a tornado warning in Oklahoma," Darlene says. I can't tell if she's talking to me or to herself. "They're advising hundreds of families to evacuate."

"Uh-huh." Usually I'd feel terrible for those people, but right now, all I can think about is what's going on inside the courtroom. Is Judge Twillings asking Mom if she'd move to Ottawa without us? Will she tell my parents I lied?

My phone, which is hidden in my backpack, vibrates. I

slide it out, hoping that Darlene, who is still reading the news, won't notice. But she does. "Your mother got you a phone?" she asks.

"No," I admit. "Grandmami did. It's probably better if you don't tell my mom."

"It's probably better if *you* tell your mom," Darlene says. "But how about I don't mention it till you do? Deal?"

"Deal."

It's a text from Mariella. *How's it going? I know it's a tough day. Your always-sister, M.*

Dad must've told her we were going to court. *Always-sister* is a message. She's saying no matter what happens, we'll always have each other. The thought makes me smile. *Thanks*, I text her back. *Your always-sister, J.*

About fifteen minutes later, the courtroom door opens. I exhale deeply. Soon all this will be over. Judge Twillings will decide what to do. Thinking about her kind eyes gives me hope that things might still end up okay.

Dad and his lawyer come out first, their faces serious.

What I see next is so awful it's hard for me to describe.

Mom, hunched over, crying. Maître Pépin patting her back and whispering something to her. Mom pushing him away.

Then Mom lifts her head and looks at me. She sobs my name.

"Justine."

I didn't even know Mom *could* cry. I've seen her stressed out and not eating. I've seen her angry. But I've never seen her cry. My heart feels like it's breaking into a million pieces.

Judge Twillings must have asked if she'd move to Ottawa without us—and Mom had to say yes. That must be why she's crying. Because she doesn't really want to go without us.

I get up. I need to go to my mom, to make her stop crying. But Darlene holds me back. "You have to stop trying to fix everything all the time, Justine," she whispers into my hair. Part of me knows she's right. I am always trying to fix things. And I haven't been doing a very good job of it.

Fred comes out next. He looks more like a grown-up than usual. For the first time I notice the fine lines on his forehead.

Darlene gets up to give Fred and me some space.

He sits down next to me. He smells like sweat. "Judge Twillings wants to see you again. To explain her decision."

"What decision?" I gulp. "Is my mom moving to Ottawa without us?"

Fred won't answer.

I gulp again. "What did Judge Twillings say?"

"Let's go and see her," Fred tells me.

Judge Twillings is waiting behind her tall desk.

She still has my pink notebook. She gestures for me to sit

down in the front row. Fred takes the seat next to mine.

I should probably wait for Judge Twillings to speak, but then I think about my mom crying, and I can't. "Please don't take us away from her!" I say. "And can you give me back my notebook? Please," I add because even if I'm upset, Judge Twillings is still a judge and I have to be polite.

She hands my notebook to the clerk, who brings it to me. "Justine," Judge Twillings says, "I have decided to make what is called an interim order—meaning it's temporary. As you know, your mother wants to take a job in Ottawa. I can't prevent her from doing that. However, I believe your home, and Beatrice's home, is in Montreal. Your school is here. Your father is here. So for the time being, I'm awarding custody to your father. You'll see your mother one night a week, and on the weekend."

"It's a stupid decision," I mutter.

Judge Twillings doesn't seem insulted. "You need to know, Justine, this isn't a decision I took lightly. As a judge, my job is to decide what's in the best interest of you and Beatr—"

"Then you should make her stay here."

Fred puts his hand on top of mine. "Let Judge Twillings finish," he whispers.

The judge is watching me with those sad eyes again. "I think Justine could use some water," she tells Fred.

Fred brings me the cup of water from the witness stand. For a second, I imagine throwing it at both of them. But I don't. I take a sip.

"The reason I reached the decision I did is that your parents can't agree. In my twenty years as a judge, I've seen that happen a lot. Parents who can't agree. It's very sad and very hard. I always wish parents could resolve things on their own"—she looks at Fred—"or with the help of lawyers. But that doesn't always happen." Judge Twillings folds her hands.

"I still don't understand," I say.

"Sometimes," Judge Twilling says, "even if parents don't mean to, they make their children feel like they're the only good parent." I nod when Judge Twillings says that. That part makes sense. For a long time, I felt like my mom was the only good parent. "And sometimes, parents make their children feel like they can't manage without them. That makes a child feel important. So important that a child might start taking—"

"Notes," I say, finishing Judge Twillings's sentence. And then I don't know why, but I add, "I like writing."

"You're an excellent writer, Justine." A compliment like that, coming from a judge, would usually make me happy, but not today.

I don't even want to imagine what it will be like to live

full-time with my dad. I'll have to remind him of everything all the time! But the look in Judge Twillings's eyes tells me she's made up her mind.

"We need our mom," I tell her. "She's our world."

"Your father is part of that world too," Judge Twillings says softly.

CHAPTER THIRTY-ONE

No one's on my side! Not Judge Twillings! Not Fred! And not my mom or dad!

I need to get out of here! I don't care if the police come after me! I don't even care if I get sent to jail. Being in jail would be better than living full-time at Dad's. The bed would definitely be more comfortable.

I push my way past Fred and run out of the courtroom into the hallway, then toward the escalator. I pass people, but I don't see their faces. It's because I'm going quickly, and also because of my own tears, which have finally come. My body heaves as I let them out.

"Justine!" I hear my dad's voice shouting.

"Justine!" That's my mother's voice.

I don't know where to go. All I know is I need to get out *now*. If only I hadn't kept notes about my dad!

I ruined everything . . . everything!

"Stop her! Stop that girl!" This time, it's both my parents' voices calling out. And Darlene's voice in the background.

Strange arms reach out to catch me. Some woman I don't know is holding on to me. "Let go!" I sob. She doesn't let go, just loosens her grip.

Then they are there—my mom and dad, talking to me at the same time.

"Everything's going to be okay, Justine. I promise." That's Dad.

"We love you." That's Mom. *We* love you?

I look into Dad's eyes, so like my own. "I don't want you to have full custody of us," I manage to say.

Mom is crying.

"I know, Justine. Your mom and I have asked for permission to speak to Judge Twillings in her chambers," Dad says. He doesn't look angry, just sad and concerned.

"What does that mean?" I spit out the words.

"It means I'm going to tell Judge Twillings I've changed my mind about Ottawa," Moms says.

Dad takes hold of my hand. "And I'm going to ask Judge Twillings to let your mother and I have joint custody. So that you and Bea could have a week with me, then a week with your mom."

I swallow my tears. "Do you think she'll say yes?" I ask.

"I don't know," Dad answers.

"What about Sheldon?"

Mom and Dad look at each other. "To be honest, with all this going on, I haven't been thinking much about Sheldon," Dad says.

I turn to Mom. Her mascara has left track marks on her cheeks. She won't be happy when she sees herself in the mirror. "Can you take Sheldon, Mom? Please."

"I don't know, honey."

"Does that mean yes?" I ask her.

Mom wipes one cheek, smearing the mascara even more. "It means I don't know."

Not long after that, I'm back in the corridor with Darlene. Mom and Dad and the lawyers are meeting with Judge Twillings.

"Do you think she'll give them joint custody?" I ask Darlene.

"I have no idea, sweetheart," Darlene says. "But I think it would be good for all of you."

Whatever Judge Twillings has to say doesn't take long. Because ten minutes later, Fred comes for me.

This time, the adults are allowed to stay in the courtroom. I sit in the same spot as before.

Judge Twillings clears her throat. "Justine, this has been a difficult day for you, and I'm sorry you had to go through all this. However, I'd like to congratulate your parents and their lawyers for working together so quickly, and for putting you and your sister first."

"Does that mean you're giving them joint custody? Oops," I add when I realize that I shouldn't have blurted that out.

"Yes, that's what it means," Judge Twillings tells me. "Starting today, your parents will have joint custody of you and Beatrice. You'll go to your father's house tonight, then to your mother's house next week."

Judge Twillings looks over her glasses at each of my parents. "I want you both to know I'll be keeping this file open for three months. If there are any applications for changes, meaning that if someone isn't respecting the conditions of my judgment"—this time, Judge Twillings looks at my mom only—"the case will come back to me.

"Things need to change," she continues. "Justine, you and your sister must feel that you are free to love both of your parents. Your mother and father might have different parenting styles, but you're lucky because you have them both."

CHAPTER THIRTY-TWO

We all file out of the courtroom together and stand in the corridor in a lopsided circle—Mom, Dad, Darlene, the lawyers and me.

Dad shifts from one foot to the other. I think even after everything that happened today, Mom still makes him nervous. "We'll need to come by and pick up the girls' stuff," he tells her. "When's a good time?"

Mom's eyes are still red from crying. "Seven o'clock," she says with a sniffle. "Seven o'clock will work."

I reach over to give Mom a hug. She hugs me back hard. "Things are going to be okay," she whispers into my hair.

"I know," I whisper back.

I turn to hug Dad. He doesn't say anything. Just rocks me in his arms.

Darlene is patting Mom's back. "I'm sorry I got angry the

other night," I hear Mom tell her. "You were right, Dar."

"Did you just apologize to me, Lisa? Or did I hear wrong?" Darlene asks.

"You heard wrong," Mom tells her.

I'm pretty sure that was a joke.

Dad and I head back to the South Shore to pick Bea up from pre-K. There's traffic on the way to the bridge. I look over at the Montreal skyline, the skyscrapers, Mount Royal in the background, and I think for a moment how lucky we are to live in this city. Dad's listening to soft rock on the radio. I turn the knob to lower the volume.

"I was keeping notes," I tell him.

"I know," he says.

"Did Judge Twillings tell you?"

Dad shakes his head. "I've known for a while." He says it quietly.

For once, I have no words.

"Your grandmami found your notebook."

"What? *Grandmami* found it? Where? That's a violation of my privacy."

Dad laughs. It's probably because I used such big words. I laugh too. After such a tough day, laughing feels like good medicine.

"That's what I told her," Dad says. "I made her promise

never, ever to do anything like that again. She promised." Dad pauses, as if he isn't sure he should say more. "She wanted me to talk to you about it."

I look at Dad. The afternoon light has landed on his forehead. "Why didn't you?"

"I didn't want to make you any more upset than you already were. I know how hard things have been for you."

I don't say anything back to that. But when we finally get onto the bridge, I think about how, if it was me, and I'd been Dad, I'd have said something—or gotten angry. Probably both.

But Dad didn't.

He did the right thing. For me. Doing the right thing matters. Even if it's hard.

I did the right thing in court today. Even if it wasn't what I planned.

I take out my phone to text Mariella. *They're going to share custody. YFS, J.* We really are forever sisters.

Bea takes the news better than I expect. She starts bopping in her seat when she learns that none of us are moving to Ottawa.

Back at Dad's, Grandmami makes us a French-style omelette with mushrooms and onions for supper. She nearly calls Dad her little boy but winks at me when she stops herself. She's also the one who tells me Dad has ordered a new bed frame and mattress for me, and that it'll be arriving before the end of the week. Maybe I won't have to go to prison to get a better bed after all.

One of these days, I'll talk to Grandmami about my notebook. But not today.

Mom calls Dad while we're having the omelette. He takes the call in the hallway and lowers his voice, but I can still hear him. "That will make the girls glad," he tells her. When he's off the phone, he explains that Mom's agreed to take Sheldon. But only on a trial basis. She told Dad he has to trim Sheldon's nails so he won't scratch the furniture. Bea starts bopping again.

After dinner, Bea and I hold Sheldon while Dad trims his nails. Then we pack up Sheldon's things—his cat toys, his litter box, his bag of dry food and his bag of treats. "Mom's going to love you," Bea tells Sheldon. "And you'll get used to her."

Mom is waiting in her lobby. She's packed our stuff in a plastic tub.

It hurts to see her standing there, all alone except for the plastic tub. She's washed the mascara off her cheeks, but her eyes are still red.

Sheldon is in his cat carrier. Dad lays the carrier down in front of Mom's feet. Bea crouches down and pokes one finger between the bars. "We'll see you next week, Sheldon," she coos. "Don't you dare scratch Mom's furniture."

Mom opens the little door at the top of the carrier and Sheldon sticks out his head. He's checking out the lobby—and Mom.

Mom pets Sheldon's nose.

She doesn't say anything about his missing eye.

Somehow, it feels like a good sign.

CHAPTER THIRTY-THREE

Living at Dad's for a whole week straight isn't easy. Even with a new bed and mattress.

Grandmami is going to Vancouver for a month to see a friend who lives there. Which means the lineup for the bathroom at Dad's won't be as long (at least not while she's away). The downside is that we'll all miss Grandmami's crazy sense of humor—and her omelettes.

Darlene told me that Judge Twillings recommended that Mom go to see a counselor. Darlene thought that was a good idea. I don't know if Mom's made an appointment yet. I hope so. But I'm not going to ask her.

I wonder sometimes if things would have turned out differently if the hearing hadn't happened so fast. Maybe it wouldn't have made a difference and Judge Twillings would still have ended up giving Mom and Dad joint custody.

I am starting to think that truth is a complicated thing.

Two people can be in the same room—or the same classroom, or the same car, or even the same courtroom—and see things totally differently. They can both be right. They can also both make mistakes sometimes.

I think that's how it is between my mom and dad.

The biggest thing I've learned is that it isn't my job to figure it all out.

ACKNOWLEDGMENTS

The word *acknowledgment* fails to convey my gratitude to my sister Carolyn Polak. She's the one who told me I had to write this book, and who, despite an unusually hectic personal and professional life, answered my endless legal questions and read multiple drafts. Thanks also to my friends Leanne Kinsella, who read an early draft and provided invaluable feedback, and Lesley Lacate, who cheered me on throughout the process. Thanks to my agent Amy Tompkins, and to Karen Li for believing in this book. Thanks to the entire team at Owlkids for bringing my story to life and for pushing me to reach deep into my characters. Thanks to my friend and editor Sarah Harvey, who once again worked her magic, helping me become a better writer. And finally, thanks to Guy Rouleau, for setting up my folding chair and making my toes twinkle.

A NOTE FROM THE AUTHOR

For a number of years, my sister Carolyn Polak, a family law lawyer, has urged me to write a novel dealing with parental alienation.

The term Parental Alienation Syndrome (PAS) was first used in 1985 by child psychiatrist Richard Gardner. Parental alienation occurs when one parent—sometimes unintentionally—turns the child or children against the other parent. It's like a chess game, in which the children became pawns.

It is estimated that this phenomenon occurs in 11 to 15 percent of all divorces involving children. This means that 1 in 10 North American children and adolescents experience it.

The *DSM-5* (*Diagnostic and Statistical Manual of Mental Disorders*), the handbook used in the United States and in many other countries around the world to diagnose mental disorders, now labels the characteristic family interactional pattern of parental alienation a form of child psychological abuse.

Sometimes parents who are experiencing great distress in their own lives do the wrong thing. It doesn't mean they're bad people or that they don't love their children. But their behavior is likely to have painful consequences for the children they love.

It's not always easy for any of us—no matter our age—to do the right thing. But we need to keep trying.

RESOURCES FOR KIDS

The following list of resources is for kids dealing with difficult situations, including parental alienation.

Your Life Your Voice—Boys Town National Hotline / www.yourlifeyourvoice.org
Trained counselors are available twenty-four hours a day, seven days a week, on this free hotline that supports American kids and teens in crisis. Call 1-800-448-3000.

Kids Help Phone / http://kidshelpphone.ca
This service is available to Canadian kids twenty-four hours a day, seven days a week. Text CONNECT to 686868 or call 1-800-668-6868 to get in touch with a trained volunteer crisis responder.

Tel-Jeunes / www.teljeunes.com
This is a confidential, free youth service program based in Quebec, available twenty-four hours a day, seven days a week. Reach them online or by telephoning 1-800-263-2266. You can also send a text to 514-600-1002, or chat with a counselor online, every day between 8 a.m. and 10:30 p.m.

RESOURCES FOR ADULTS

The list of online resources below is for parents and professionals seeking to help youngsters dealing with the effects of divorce and parental alienation.

Carrefour Aliénation Parentale /
https://alienationparentale.ca/en/association
This website was created by parents and professionals to help families recognize, prevent and put a stop to parental alienation.

National Parent Hotline / www.nationalparenthelpline.org
This US-based organization believes asking for help is a sign of strength. Operated by Parents Anonymous, this telephone hotline provides emotional support from trained advocates. Call 1-855-4A-PARENT.

Banana Splits Resource Center /
www.bananasplitsresourcecenter.org
This is a school-based program to help kids deal with their parents' divorce, or the death of a parent.

Parental Alienation Awareness Organization / www.paaousa.org

This organization works to raise awareness and open discussion about parental alienation.

Youth Mental Health Canada / https://ymhc.ngo

YMHC is a non-profit organization that provides mental wellness resources for Canadian youth.